Crimson Dust

The Tuscarora Trail ran for a hundred miles through the wind-scoured, sandy Arizona badlands. Here, the country was battered apart by sweeping winds, and the whole vastness dissolved into a surging crimson dust. Covering every trail, threatening to choke every living thing that was in its path, the whirling sand whipped at men's faces, sticking to their skin, grinding into their eyes, distorting their very reason with its madness.

One such sandstorm was starting to rage when Jeff Denver rode into this red wilderness. The trail he had been following for ten days was rapidly disappearing under the shifting sands. With dreadful certainty Jeff knew that the trail would be lost within minutes and he knew too that the men he had been following would have crossed the badlands by now.

They would be waiting for him, guns at the ready and, one way or another, an early death looked likely to be Jeff's destiny.

Crimson Dust

Cliff Daventry

A Black Horse Western

ROBERT HALE · LONDON

© 1966, 2003 John Glasby
First hardcover edition 2003
Originally published in paperback as
Gallows High by Tex Bradley

ISBN 0 7090 7242 2

Robert Hale Limited
Clerkenwell House
Clerkenwell Green
London EC1R 0HT

Typeset by
Derek Doyle & Associates, Liverpool.
Printed and bound in Great Britain by
Antony Rowe Limited, Wiltshire

CHAPTER 1

BADLAND TRAIL

Like a bone, bleached white by having been too long out in the sun, the dried-up bed of the river stretched away to the north and south. At its margin, where the banks had been eaten away in years gone by, the embankments formed a ragged windbreak, the white alkali dunes gathered together in high drifts, and it was these, more than the sun-baked earth, which defined the winding course of the riverbed. At intervals, the clumps of green-brown cactus marked the distance of a concealed ridge from the river, or the stump of a withered tree stood guard over an empty creek, once a narrow tributary of the river itself.

For several hours, since dawn that day, Jeff Denver had been forced to endure a purgatory on earth, the undiluted hell of light and heat which were the Badlands during the day. There had been scarcely a breath of wind all morning and his tracks, since he had ridden down from the wide ledge which was the only uplifted stretch of ground as far as the eye could see, were clearly visible in the white dust.

Under the brassy silent sky, the dunes ran on for miles. Seldom varying more than a few feet from trough to crest, they glared fiercely in the strong sunlight, shimmered like water far out near the horizon. Nowhere was there a well-defined margin between the desert and the trail he was following. At intervals, he had ridden past the skeleton of a Conestoga wagon, the spars thrusting out of the dust like curved, wooden ribs. These were mute, but forceful reminders that many of the people who had travelled this way in the past had never made it.

Resting his mount, he smoked a handmade cigarette, sitting forward in the saddle. He was low on water, had hoped to find some here, but now, with the river dry, he would have to ride an unguessable distance before he came to any more. Lifting his canteen to his ear, he shook it slightly. Half full, he reckoned. Enough to take him another day or so, but not much further. How his mount would fare was a problem he would soon have to face.

Finishing his cigarette, he flicked the spent butt into the dust, gigged his mount forward. It moved reluctantly, nosing its way over the riverbed, up the far bank and into the dunes which stretched like an endless sea of sand out to the horizon. It was now almost high noon and the heat was fierce and blistering. The sun blazed down from the cloudless heavens and the ground around the river formed a natural amphitheatre which seemed to collect and hold the heat. It was a punishing, burning pressure on his back and shoulders; and on the rolling flatness of the desert, coiling back from the scorched ground so that it formed a thin, just-seen turbulence all about him, bringing with it the rendered-out smell of the sage and bitter mesquite.

The three men he had been trailing for some days now had taken this route across the Flats, were perhaps three days ride ahead of him. For a moment, he felt the urgency building up inside him again, but thrust it down with a conscious effort. Those men would keep on riding until they reached the mountains on the far edge of the Badlands, simply because there was no other place hereabouts where they could ride. He felt certain they would not backtrack in the hope of throwing him off their trail and to turn north or south would mean at least a week longer in the desert. They would continue west by the only trail possible and if he could move fast, he might reach the other side before they had time to set up an ambush for him.

By now, they would know he was riding behind them, ever since he had raised a smell of them back at one of the line camps he had ridden through, almost fifty miles east of the Flats. The description given him by the men there had tallied exactly with what he remembered of them from a year back. Then, they had ridden with him in a detachment of cavalry in the defeated Army of the South. All three had volunteered to scout the enemy's forward positions and acting on the information they brought back, he had ordered his men forward, only to ride into a well-planned enemy ambush. He had lost almost every man under his command, had been wounded himself in the action.

When he had come round in the small ward of the field hospital, he had learned that he was to be court-martialled for what had happened. His final discharge from the Army, two months before the signing of the peace at Appomattox Courthouse had been an ignominious one, bringing disgrace on himself and his family. His evidence concerning the information brought back by Ed Denson, Matt Woodrow and Reno Kearney had not been believed at his trial; but it had not been for another six months that he had learned the truth of what had really happened. Until then, he had not thought of the possibility of treachery on the part of those three men. Then, little things had become apparent. The fact that none of these men had been with the detachment when they had ridden into that ambush, that shortly after they had left the Army once peace had been brought to a divided country, all three had suddenly acquired wealth in the form of Union dollars, that all had been offered posts with the Union Army in the South, but had refused them to ride out west.

He rubbed the sweat from his forehead, wrinkling his eyes where the irritating sand had worked its way into the folds of his skin. Once he had made up his mind about these three men, the seed of hate had been sown in his brain giving him no peace. He had sold everything to buy a thoroughbred horse, a rifle, two Colts and the few items looped around his saddle. The bitter memory of that hot, sultry morning still lived in his thoughts, something which could never be erased. Firmly etched on his brain were the mutilated bodies of his men, strewn around the thickets where they had been cut down by the massed, murderous fire from well-entrenched Yankee positions. Now that he was free of the Army, knowing that nothing he could do would bring back his honour, tracking down these three traitors was the only thing which fired his ambition. It was the one dominant thought that overrode everything else in his mind, the only thing which drove him on from one day to the next, enabling him to face and overcome all of the dangers and discomforts of this long trail west. Sooner, or later, he told himself fiercely, savagely, those three men would stand in front of his gun and would know whose finger it was that pulled the trigger which blasted them into eternity.

Three weeks earlier, after losing sight of them for more than a month, he had picked up their trail once more in Fort Cranton, had lost it again several times, only to run across a whisper of them at the various line camps scattered throughout this part of the frontier. Once they had pulled out of that last camp, heading in the direction of the Flats, he had found trailing them more easy than before. But he had been made cautious by the fact that in conversation with the men at the camp, it had transpired that the three men had dropped hints of a man who might be trailing them, had asked the men to be on the look out for him.

With the sun middle-down, he rested again for half an hour among jagged rocks, but with the rolling flatness of the desert still stretched out in front of him, the low heat haze concealing most of the details. The long rim of rocks which he had hoped to cross before sundown still appeared to be about fifteen or twenty miles ahead of him and as soon as he was moving again, he went on at the best possible speed, travelling swiftly westward towards the sun as if there was a time check on him.

The hours passed slowly, long tormented things. The heat had increased during the afternoon until it seemed that he was forcing his way through a burning sea of air which gave him no respite. Every breath he took was an effort that forced a gust of burnt, superheated air down into his heaving, tortured lungs. A strange sense of dejection settled over him as he swayed in the saddle.

Gradually, however, the sun lowered itself down towards the distant rim of ground. The harsh, brassy glare faded from the inverted bowl of the heavens and the deeper reds and crimsons began to seep into the sky to the west. The horse, too, was beginning to feel the faint diminution in the heat for it picked up its gait a little as though anxious to be out of this terrible wilderness that wanted nothing of man or animal. Its previous sloth-like step became one of jauntiness.

Choosing the southern wall of the rim, where there was a little shade from the sun, he kept a sharp eye open for breaks in the sheer wall of rock that slanted across the desert, long and monotonous. The sun was finally setting when he rode along a sandy ledge on to a low shelf of ground. Beyond, the flatness of the desert stretched away to the dark skyline with nothing to break the emptiness unless—

There was a small-shaped blur over to his right, a square

of darker shadow which stood out starkly from the rest of the terrain, so starkly that it attracted his attention right away, drawing his gaze irresistibly towards it. It was undoubtedly a ranch headquarters, a little way off the direct route across the Flats. Narrowing his eyes, he watched it closely for a little while, then noticed the small cloud of dust to the left of the cluster of buildings, a signal of one or more riders moving fast through the sand. He kept his gaze riveted on that dust for a few minutes and finally reached the conclusion that it was a single rider spurring his mount in the direction of the ranch.

His previous intention had been to continue riding until dark; then find a suitable place in which to make night camp, but the discovery of this ranch, isolated out here in this wilderness, made him change his mind. At least he might sleep dry and warm, and there would surely be water there for his mount.

He reckoned it would take him the best part of an hour to reach the ranch and he sat forward in the saddle, sitting easy, even-balanced to save the horse. As he rode, his eyes lidded a little against the vivid red glow of the sunset, he fell to wondering why a man should live out here, so far from the main trail and from any of the comforts and amenities. Life here would be so hard and difficult that it almost did not bear thinking about. Only a man on the run, anxious to avoid contact with his fellow men, would ever think of living out here, he reasoned.

The rider he had spotted had long since vanished by the time he rode through the shifting sand towards the ranch. As he drew nearer he saw that it was, in reality, a smaller place than he had thought. Just a couple of low-roofed buildings set back-to-back and a smaller place off to one side, big enough to house a couple of horses, but not much more.

He had reined up in the middle of the courtyard, a square patch of dust, and was on the point of dismounting when the door opened and a man stepped out on to the small wooden porch. He was short and thick-set, chalked in alkali dust, his broad features puffed with heat, marking him out as the man who had just ridden in from the desert. There was a Springfield in his hands, the barrel laid squarely on Denver's chest.

'Just hold it right there, mister,' he said harshly. There was a sharp note of suspicion in his tone and his eyes watched Denver shrewdly. 'If you've got any business here, get it done with, and then ride on.'

Denver kept his hands well away from the guns at his waist as he contemplated the other closely. He could imagine anyone being a mite suspicious of a stranger, but this hostile inhospitality was something he had never expected. He moved his hands slowly, dug into his shirt pocket and brought out his tobacco pouch, made a cigarette slowly, licked it, then thrust it between his lips without lighting it.

'You're sure a heap touchy, ain't you?' he said finally. 'Scared of somethin'? Can't imagine what it could be, way out here off the trail.'

The other narrowed his eyes, came forward a couple of paces. The barrel of the gun did not waver an inch, rock steady in his hands, his finger bar-straight on the trigger.

A dog, long and lean, its hair lank, scuffled around the corner of the building, lifted its head to stare up at Denver, teeth bared in a snarl.

'You look like the same breed as those other three who rode through here a few days back,' grunted the other harshly. His lids crept closer together, somehow enhancing the beady brightness of his eyes.

'Not quite,' Denver said. He lit the cigarette, blew the smoke through his nostrils in twin streams.

'Then you don't deny knowin' them.'

'No. Sounds as if they're the same three I've been trailin' for a long time now.' He sat easy in the saddle now,

11

with one leg just hooked over the saddlehorn. 'What sort of yarn did they spin you?'

'That there might be a hired killer after them.'

'Anythin' else?'

'That you're fixin' to do this because of some grudge you got against them.' He laid his glance on Denver like the edge of a razor, bright and motionless but needing little for it to cut. This man was the lone sort, Jeff reflected inwardly, maybe forced on the run some years before, now cutting himself off from the rest of the world, answering to no one and responsible only to what little conscience he had.

'Do you hold with murder, mister?' Denver asked pointedly. He met the other's gaze head-on.

The other hesitated, then shook his head stolidly.

'I figured not. Maybe there's somethin' way back in your past that made you come out here and live like this; maybe you had nothin' to do with the war. But men did a lot of bad things then and those three men were the worst I knew.'

Silence settled for a long moment between the two men. The older man shifted where he stood, seemed undecided, considered Jeff thoughtfully, then he scowled. 'What sort of thing did they do, mister?'

'They betrayed me and my men to the enemy, scouted ahead of us, and then took Yankee gold to lead us into an ambush. I lost most of my men that day, lost my honour too. I swore then that I'd ride those traitors down and kill them and I still mean to do that.'

Slowly, the other lowered the gun in his hands. 'A man can get fooled,' he said softly, 'but to me you talk like a man who speaks the truth.' He gestured with a thumb. 'Water's round at the back of the house. You can put your horse into the barn yonder with mine for the night. Reckon you'll be wantin' to ride out at sun-up tomorrow.'

Jeff nodded, slid from the saddle, stretching his long,

lean body to ease the digging fingers of cramp which lanced through his limbs. He felt stiff and saddle sore as he loosened the cinch, pulled the bridle slowly off the horse's head, then led it round the side of the house to where a small trough stood with a trickle of clear water coming from the pipe which ran into the ground. There was a small well there, he guessed, with the water helped to the surface by the grating sails of the windmill which turned slowly, listlessly. How long it would work considering the lack of breeze in this terrible country was a question he could not answer, but he bent and slaked his thirst, letting the warmish water trickle down his throat and into his belly. He felt all twisted and warped inside like a board that had been left too long out in the sun, becoming brittle with the hours and days.

When he was finished and his horse had drunk, he led it into the small barn, then walked over to the ranch house where the other was waiting for him. He followed the oldster inside, waited as the other propped his rifle in one corner of the room.

'The name's Jeff Denver,' he said quietly, extending his hand. 'One-time lieutenant in the Confederate Army. Drummed out at court-martial for leading my men into that ambush I told you about.'

The other gave a quick jerk of his head. 'Leaher,' he said tersely, shaking Jeff's hand. 'Sam Leaher. Like you guessed, I had nothin' to do with the war. I've been too busy stayin' out of the way of the law to have had time to worry about that.'

Jeff glanced about him. There was a small cook stove just visible in the other room, a bed in the corner of the room in which he stood. Everywhere there were signs of hard times. Living out here in this wilderness, Jeff would have expected nothing else. How the other managed to survive was little short of a miracle. The spring out back of the house must have been the only one within a distance of more than fifty miles. If it should ever run dry, then this man was in real trouble.

'This ain't much,' said the other, noticing the direction of his glance, 'but I like it. Not many visitors here. Most men ridin' west take the trail to the north, around the perimeter of the Flats.'

'Guess I'd have done the same if I wasn't followin' a trail,' Jeff agreed. 'You say those three men are just a few days or so ahead of me.'

'That's right. They must have spotted this place as you did. Were short of water when they got here. But they didn't ride up and ask for it like you did. They came on me just after dark, held me up at gunpoint. One of the reasons I figure you're tellin' the truth about this matter.'

The other moved off into the other room. 'I'll fix us some grub,' he called a moment later. 'Won't be much, but it'll be better than an empty stomach.'

Jeff ate ravenously when the meal was set down to him. From across the table, Leaher watched him, poured a second cup of steaming coffee from the jug.

'You've been ridin' far, Denver,' he observed. 'You've got that look about you. This ain't the best sort of country to trail men through.'

Jeff shrugged, drained the cup of coffee, set it down on the table in front of him. 'Hasn't been too bad so far, apart from the heat and the lack of water out there.'

'There's going to be a change soon,' opined the other. He took out a battered pipe, began thrusting the brown strands of tobacco into it, pressing it down into the bowl with his thumb. 'It's about this time that the norther picks up. There were signs of it in the sky tonight at sundown; a mite too red looking, clouds startin' to bank up on the horizon.'

'That bad?' Jeff inquired.

'If you'd lived here as long as I have, you'd know just how bad it is. Tonight – maybe by tomorrow mornin', the wind is goin' to start up, sweepin' down from the north, bringin' all the sand and dust with it, dust so goddamned thick you can't see your horse's ears in front of you even if you bend forward in the saddle, and it blows that way for days on end, without lettin' up once. I've known men ride out in it and get lost within half an hour of leavin' here, ride around in circles until we find 'em once the storm dies down, half-buried under the sand, stiff and dead. Ain't nothin' worth losin' your life for in these storms.'

'There are some things a man has to do, even if it means riskin' his own life,' Jeff said slowly, solemnly. 'If I don't ride out now, I'll lose their trail and they'll have time to set up a trap for me on the other side of the Flats.'

'It's as important to you as that?' muttered the other.

'Afraid so.' Jeff gave a quick nod. He settled back in his chair, his legs stretched out straight in front of him beneath the table.

Leaher paused for a moment and then nodded his head very slowly. 'I reckon I can understand what it is that drives a man to do these things. A man like me don't know much about which side is right and which is wrong but, by tarnation, I know snakes when I see 'em.'

'And you. What made you have to come out here, shut-tin' yourself off from everybody?'

For a moment it was as if the other had not heard the question. Then he said softly, choosing his words carefully. 'It was all a long time ago, more'n twenty years now. There was a little town close to the Texas border. Some drunken cowpoke, whooping it up, rode down my sister in the street, laughed while he did it. She died the same day without even gainin' consciousness. I waited until dark, then I found this drunk in the saloon, told him who I was, why I meant to kill him. I didn't carry a gun in those days and he saw that, must've figured I was unarmed for he went for his gun a little slow. But I had a knife and that was more'n enough. I could hit a fly at twenty paces with a knife,

15

Denver. That was somethin' this *hombre* evidently didn't know. I had that knife in his throat before he could pull his gun clear of leather.'

'And you started on the run because of that?'

'It was a town run by cattlemen. The sheriff was paid by the ranchers. I never had a chance of justice. I'd have been strung up without a trial if I'd waited around. But I lit out of there and kept on ridin', takin' any trail I found myself on. Then I came out here, knew it was the very spot where nobody would come lookin' for me. I've been here for close on ten years now, keeping away from the trails, just eking out an existence. Reckon it's no more'n I can really hope for. At least, I'm still alive.'

Jeff eyed the other across the table in the pale, flickering yellow glow of the lantern. Inwardly, he judged the other to be no better and no worse than a hundred other men he had met, both during the war and after it. Men who had encountered one rotten break in their lives which had either sent them to the wild bunch who roamed the hills and plains of the frontier States, or into isolation as had happened with Sam Leaher. He thought about that for a while and was troubled inwardly. The thought that maybe his own future was to be shaped this way by destinies over which he had very little, if any, control, burdened him oppressively.

'They got you chased out of this town and because of that you can't ride like other men. You've got to sweat it out in this wild wilderness, with only the heat and the sand to keep you company. Why don't you up and leave it, ride on to the west where nobody knows you now and where there's a good chance that the smell of gunsmoke has worn off. Find yourself some outfit and work for them for a year or so and then you'll be able to ride free, take any trail you want, go into a saloon in some strange town and sit with your back to the door without bein' afraid or wonderin' if a bullet might come

16

through the doorway with your name etched on its leaden hide.'

The other pondered that for a moment then shook his head sadly. 'Could be that a few years ago I might have risked it, but not now. It's too late now. Ain't many more years left to me and I'd like to make 'em as many as possible without lookin' for trouble.'

'It's your life,' Jeff said, shrugging. 'How you run it is your business. I guess you know best.' He filled up his cup from the coffee pot, poured in a little of the milk from the tin, stirred it, then drank it down. Some of the weariness left his body and he got up from the table, scraping back his chair.

'Reckon I'll just see to my horse,' he said quietly. Outside, it was already dark, and the stars shone brilliantly in the clear velvet heavens, so close he felt he had only to reach up with his fingers to brush his hands across them. The barn was a dark shadow in front of him and he went inside, watered his mount, fed it a little of the hay from the meagre stock at the back of the building, then stepped outside again, drawing in great lungfuls of the cold night air. The temperature dropped suddenly and sharply in the desert once the sun went down.

As he stood there, he stared off to the north, felt the faint breeze on his face, coming from that direction. Maybe Leaher had been right when he reckoned there was going to be a sudden change in the weather. He scanned the flat northern horizon, looking for some sign, and saw it almost at once, where the clouds, faint and filmy, were just beginning to obscure the stars low down near the skyline.

It would be just his bad luck, he thought bitterly, for the norther to start to blow now, just when he was on the last lap of his journey. He had faced the bitterness of losing these men too often in the past to want to face it again, knew that come what may, he would have to ride out first thing the next morning, heading into whatever nature might have in store for him.

That night, the long days on the trail finally caught up with him and when he stretched himself out on the bunk, the lumpy, hard-pitted mattress seemed as soft and as luxurious as down to his weary body. He shut his eyes and turned his thoughts towards the three men on the trail somewhere ahead of him, trying for a moment to gauge where they might be at that moment. If they had already crossed the Flats and were in the greener country on the other side, then the coming storm would have no effect on them, would almost certainly be to their advantage, slowing him up, giving them more time in which to make their preparations for his death. The idea troubled him and he thought: 'I've got to ride and make good time tomorrow, storm or not.' He tried to continue his train of thought, but his mind, numbed by the utter weariness, refused to obey him and he slept.

A hand, flat on his chest, woke him up and he opened his eyes to find the oldster standing over him, staring down at him in the grey light, of an early dawn.

'You slept hard durin' the night,' said the other, as Jeff swung his legs to the floor and thrust himself to his feet. 'Even the sound of the wind didn't wake you.'

Jeff rubbed the stubble on his chin, stared about him for a moment, and then grew aware of the dismal moan of the wind around the corners of the house, whining and whistling as it sought out, and discovered, the cracks in the wooden planks, tiny piles of red sand forming along the walls where it was being carried inside.

'Seems to me you were right about the storm,' he said dully.

Leaher gave a brief nod. 'Signs are unmistakable. You still set on ridin' out into that? It's goin' to grow a heap worse before midday.'

Jeff buckled on his gunbelt, hitched it up an inch or so, ran his fingers over the butts of the guns in the holsters, then nodded. 'No man can ever wipe the slate clean, my friend. Sometimes he has to do things he dislikes.'

Leaher eyed him closely for a moment, then turned away. 'I'll get you a bite to eat before you ride out. No tellin' when you'll get another.'

When he had left the room, Jeff moved over to the window and stared out into the greying dawn. The sand was scudding around the lean-to near the barn, piling high in drifts against the bottom of the walls and it was impossible to see the horizon. He withdrew his head from the window, pulled on his boots, then went through into the other room. The smell of frying bacon reached him from the small kitchen.

When Leaher came in with the breakfast, he laid his glance on Jeff, as grave as the other had seen him, watching him in a searching way – reading what his face might hold, then looked away. He drew in his breath, then let it out softly.

'You goin' to kill these men when you catch up with 'em?' he asked.

'That's right.' There was no emotion in Jeff's voice; he was simply stating a fact. 'I've waited a long time for this. There's no goin' back now.'

'How do you reckon this chore will leave you, always assumin' that you manage to live through it?'

'That's somethin' I haven't stopped to think about.'

'Don't you think you ought to?'

'No!' Jeff shook his head sharply, almost angrily, at the suggestion. 'This may not be easy for you to understand, but those men who rode with me that day, trusted me; I was responsible for them, everyone. The ghosts of those who died in that ambush have haunted me every second of every day since then, and they'll go on haunting me until I kill the men who betrayed us. Not until I've finished this chore will I really be free.'

'So you have to go on no matter what happens,' nodded the other. He motioned to Jeff's cup, filled it again with the hot coffee at the other's brief nod. Cocking his head a little on one side, he said: 'That storm out there is goin' to get a hell of a lot worse before the mornin' is through. And it'll go on for three or more days before it starts to die down. Is it worth riskin' your life like this, just for the sake of a few days? If you die in that sand and wind, you'll never finish this chore.'

'If I don't ride out now, I'll never find their trail. I've missed it too often in the past to want to run that risk again.' He drained the coffee quickly even though the hot liquid scalded the back of his throat on the way down, pushed back his chair, and rose hastily to his feet.

'Thanks for your hospitality, Sam. I never expected anythin' like this out here in the desert.'

'And you won't find anythin' else like it until you get to the other side of the Flats,' said the other seriously. He got to his feet, moved around the corner of the table and followed Jeff to the door. The wind sighed round the house and then rose swiftly up a saw-edged scale until it was shrieking thinly in their ears and when Jeff thrust open the door, he felt the resistance of it against his arm. Sand threw itself into his face as he stepped out on to the porch where several of the slatted wooden boards were already silted up with the red sand. A million grains blotted out all sight of the sun, yet there was a growing heat in the air which could be felt.

Bringing his horse from the barn, he threw on the saddle, bent to tighten the cinch, then checked the rifle in its scabbard before swinging up. Leaher was still standing in the doorway, one hand up to his face, shielding his eyes against the growing fury of the storm. Jeff lifted a hand in farewell, then touched spurs to his mount's flanks, tightened his grip on the reins and bent low in the saddle and urged his horse forward into the teeth of the norther that moaned over the Flats, lifting the irritating grains of sand from the creases of the ridges, hurling them through the air.

Tying his bandana over his nose and mouth, he narrowed his eyes to mere slits, striving to make out any sort of trail in front of him. The eagerness was still in him, a force which drove him on, but although he raked spurs over the animal's flanks, it refused to travel any faster; almost as though it realised that there was only danger and discomfort lying ahead of them. The wind continued to lift once the sun came up and it was just possible to make out the fiery disc through the swirling clouds of sand, glaring redly and ominously through the hazy dust. Within an hour, his mount was soaked in lather and sweat but he continued to push it as quickly as possible. It rolled in its stride, its breathing a sobbing, heavy sound which he could hear clearly even above the undulating shriek of the wind.

They crossed a patch of broomweed that somehow managed to survive in the terrible conditions, clattered among rocks which thrust themselves out of the more level ground, rocks which had now been scoured clean of dust, their smooth surfaces shining faintly in the hazy sunlight. Riding in and out of the stony gulches and arroyos, scattering rock and pebbles underfoot, sending them rolling and bouncing down the slopes, he rode heedless of the discomfort. The sand had now worked its way between his clothing and his flesh, scraping and itching; his boots were full of it, the folds of his skin burned where it had forced its way into the tiny crevices and mingled with the sweat that poured down his cheeks and forehead. His eyes had been scoured by it, lids tender and smarting intolerably. He filled his lungs with a deep breath that burned deep within his chest, forced his head up to face the wind and stared through the red haze in front of him, striving to make out details; but everything seemed indistinct and blurred by the dust storm, the limit of his visibility less than twenty yards now and there was no sign at all of the wind abating. The wind seemed to be inter- mittent now, not always blowing from the same direction so that it was impossible to protect himself from the full fury of it. Gradually, the fear that he might, after all, be riding in circles, rose in his mind and grew stronger as the hours passed. Long, tortuous things, the minutes were drawn out into an endless sense of pain, of struggling to draw breath. By now, the bandana no longer acted as a filter. The tiny pores were clogged with the probing sand, making every breath a tremendous effort.

Ahead of him, the terrain was changing. Through the millions of swirling, gritty particles he was able to make out the tall basaltic formations that lifted on either side of the trail, looming like huge, ghostly fingers out of the crimson gloom They seemed like grim sentinels, piled in a nightmare confusion so that it was impossible for him to use any of them as landmarks to find his direction. Even the sun, seen intermittently through the gloom was of little help. The trail, which he had managed to follow in places, was now all but obliterated. The drifting sand filled in all of the hollows, smoothing out the ground between the rocks.

Shortly after midday, he reined up in the shelter of one of the tall, rising rocks, dismounting and pressing himself in against the rough base where there was a little shelter from the swirling dust. The wind still keened in his ears and the dusty rattle of the sand against the rocks blotted out all other sounds. With no cooling effect due to the cloud of flying sand, the rocks around him reflected the heat of the sun like banks of ash from some huge furnace and he seemed to be suspended in some timeless world with only the faint, diffuse shadow of the rock on the sand, adjusting its length and perimeter, reminding him of the slow movement of the dimly seen sun.

He ate a little of the food he had brought with him, poured some of the water into his hat and gave it to the horse. It was not as much as the animal wanted, nor for that matter did he drink much himself, but the worst of the day was yet to come and it was better to ride dry through the heat than to lash out a lot of sweat.

Half an hour later, he moved out, crossed through a narrow pass between two sheer-rising walls of rock, down a slippery slope, treacherous now that the sand had become silted up by the wind, into flatter country, leaving the rocks behind. All around him, everything was featureless, with no landmarks to break the stretching monotony. At times he thought the storm was dying down. The wind would diminish to a faintly heard moan and the scudding clouds of sand appeared to be settling, but the respite was only temporary. Within minutes, fresh gusts would sweep down from a northerly direction, whipping up the grains once more, hurling them in stinging waves at every exposed part of his body. It was impossible to find a comfortable position in the saddle. The sand had rubbed his flesh raw and there was blood on his face whenever he rubbed at an itching spot.

Now there was no cover to break the force of the wind, no shelter from the sand and from its throbbing whine, the wind rose to an ear-splitting shriek which wailed at his ears until they hurt with the roar of it. Eyes screwed up, the edges of his jacket whipping at his sides, he urged the horse forward, forced to keep a tight rein on the animal, to keep it heading into the wind. In the blinding, merciless haze that needled him continually, his progress was much slower than he had hoped. Nightfall found him traversing a wide ledge of rock which jutted out from an otherwise flat plain. Smoothed by the wind, the red sandy dunes covered the edge of the ridge like waves on a motionless ocean, throwing up only a reddish spray. The sand was smooth and unmarked and he rode through it, tensed and cautious in spite of himself.

Darkness brought a coolness to the wind which whipped up the stinging clouds of sand, but no respite from the storm itself. He was still pointed towards the west as far as he was able to determine, but within fifteen minutes, the ledge began to climb, not steeply, but in steps, an area which had been roughened and twisted by some long-gone geological upheaval which had taken this stretch of ground and warped it into incredible shapes. A pathway showed briefly through gaps in the scudding sand, dipping steeply down the side of the precipice on his left and he debated whether to take it. It was a moment of decision. If he stayed here near the summit of the ledge, he would be exposed to the full, blasting fury of the storm throughout the night. If he took the dangerous, downward track he might find it impossible to go on after a little while, but if it did lead him down to somewhere near the base of this ridge, he would at least have some shelter.

At length, not altogether freed from doubt, he put his mount to the downgrade, straightening his legs, thrusting them stiffly against the stirrups to check the forward slide of the horse, and rode into the descending face of the ridge.

CHAPTER 2

MAN WITH A GRUDGE

The next day brought no let-up in the fury of the storm and it was not until late in the afternoon of the third day that Jeff noticed a change in the burning touch of the wind on his face. At first, the change was so slight that it passed unnoticed, but then he gradually grew aware that the wind was dying. The fact penetrated his numbed mind slowly. As it was, his first thought was that this was just another trick of the storm, that it would start up again in a few minutes, hurl itself at him from a different direction. But as the minutes passed and the wind still continued to drop, he felt hope return to his mind. He lifted his head, stared out into the red-brown clouds of dust which swirled a little more slowly about him. His flesh felt as though it had been rubbed raw, his eyes smarted intolerably so that he could scarcely bear to open them.

Almost directly ahead of him, the sun appeared for the first time. This was one of the miracles of these sandstorms which blew up along the Flats. One moment the air was filled with the swirling grains, and the next it was clear.

The wind dropped. The dust settled almost at once and there was a vivid blue sky showing in front of him, with the sun blazing down from it, throwing lengthening shadows over the desert.

Wearily, he rubbed the back of his hand over his forehead, winced as the dust which had formed a thick red mask on his face, ground into the raw, abraded skin. Squinting into the clear, cloudless heavens, he tried to judge the time, reckoned it was close on five o'clock, with the heat head still high in its piled-up intensity. But anything was better than the shrieking wind and sand and he drew in his first breath of clear air for what seemed an eternity.

There was a range of low hills stretching across the horizon and he judged them to be less than ten miles distant. Riding slowly down a rock-bound descent, he entered rougher ground, less inviting in spite of the clear air. It was a strange place of weird buttes, stretches of deep sand and steep-sided gorges cut in the earth by wind and water. Beyond them lay mesquite and cactus and then, two miles further on, stunted scrub oak which gave him an advance indication of what was to come once he reached the hills. Pursing his lips, he reckoned that with luck he might reach the hills before nightfall and dug spurs into the horse's flanks, to urge it forward. It increased its pace gallantly, head lifted a little higher. A thoroughbred, it had survived the rigours of the storm far better than most other animals would have done.

The sun went down while he was still a couple of miles from the low hills, dropping beyond them into a vivid splash of flame which lit up the entire western heavens like some vast explosion in another world. Darkness fell swiftly and by the time he rode through the huge boulders which marked the entrance into the hills, the first stars were beginning to glitter down in the east and he realised that it would not be long before his sight failed him and he would have to look around for a suitable place to make camp.

A quarter of a mile inside the hills, he came on a high, rocky wall which reared up to his right and there was the beginnings of a trail, just visible in front of him. He balanced himself evenly in the saddle, rolled himself a smoke and lit it, drawing the smoke deeply into his lungs. It was the first cigarette he had really enjoyed since leaving Sam Leaher's ranch house.

There was a narrow defile in the rock face and he rode into it, following it for half mile before it widened into a steep upward path. At the top, he rode among gigantic boulders which loomed high above him at every turn, then came down into a wide, but shallow basin, sheltered on all sides, with some rough grass in it, some bushes and a few stunted trees. There was also a thin trickle of water that flowed sluggishly through the basin, then dipped over the southern lip and went plunging down the side at an ever-increasing pace.

Stopping here, he put the horse on a picket in the short grass, built himself a fire and cooked the last of the food he had brought with him in his saddlebag from Leaher's. It meant he would be forced to start out hungry in the morning, but he guessed that by now, he was close to some town or ranch where he could get something to eat within an hour or so of continuing his journey. He felt no fear of his fire being seen by anyone in the vicinity. He was high up here and because of this, the walls of the basin, although low, were sufficient to protect him from sight by anyone down on the trail. The wind too, blowing soft and cool off the ragged summits, would take his smoke along the lee of the ridge, away from the trail.

But even so, he made up his blankets on the very rim of the firelight, tossed more twigs on to the fire, waited for the flames to build up, then moved away, stretched

27

himself out under the blankets and rolled over on to his side, slipping his guns under the saddle he used for a pillow.

He woke to grey dawn, but by the time he had rolled up his blankets and tied them securely on to the saddle, kicked out the remains of the fire and swung up into the saddle, the dawn was streaking the far horizons with red and gold and the sun came bounding up behind the low clouds as he rode out of the basin, down through the trees and rocks and into a wide pass that led him all the way through the hills and out into a lush green valley that lay beyond.

His movements were wary now, his eyes alert for danger. This was, he guessed, the trail those three men had used once they had ridden across the Flats and there was just the chance that one at least of them had stayed behind to watch the trail for a few days, ready to jump him the moment he showed up. Only that way could they feel really sure and safe.

When he reached timber on the edge of the valley, he moved into it, off the trail, riding parallel to the road but a quarter of a mile from it. At times, through breaks in the trees, he was able to see it clearly, a little way below him, a grey scar against the greenness, but there were no riders on it, no travellers moving in either direction.

The horse slowed frequently now, knowing its own mind and he did not push it, having the feeling that he was nearing the end of the trail, that a few more hours would make little difference compared with all of the time which had passed.

There was a ranch off in the distance when he rode out of the trees, and he skirted around it, sighting the perimeter wire on two occasions, steering well clear of it. Until he knew the whereabouts of the three men he was hunting, he did not intend to give away his presence in the territory. A little later, he swung down from the hills, crossed the main trail again and in spite of having seen and heard no one during the morning, the sharp smell of dust, lifted by horse's hoofs hung in the air, biting at the back of his nostrils, warning of other travellers criss-crossing the territory and against the background of silence of the hills he had the impression of vague, faintly-heard tag-ends of sound which had not quite faded out into the overall stillness.

He crossed a wide meadow, moved down through the thickly tangled vegetation which grew in lush profusion along the bank of a swift-flowing river, turned his mount into the water and let it swim over to the far side. It was here, at this point, that he caught the faint break of gunfire in the distance, reaching across to him from the north. He reined up his horse, leaned forward in the saddle, listening intently. The sound of shots came and went on the breeze which blew along the river, funnelled by the high banks of undergrowth.

The gunfire came in sharp volleys, heavy at times and then fading almost into silence. For a moment, he debated his position, then reached a sudden decision, swung his mount around sharply and kicked it into a rapid trot that carried them swiftly along the river bank, out of the trees a little while later, over a green meadow, through more timber and finally out on to a ridge that looked down on to a narrow valley which shimmered faintly in the heat haze that was drawing all of the moisture out of the ground.

Narrowing his eyes against the sun glare, he looked about him. The firing had died away now and a deep, pendant silence had settled over the scene. There was a small settlement at the far end of the valley and even from where he sat, he could make out the plots of cultivated ground, guessed that it had been taken over by homesteaders. Knowing the bitter rivalry and antagonism that existed between the ranchers and the nesters in this part of the territory, he felt reasonably confident that the gunfire had come from down there.

He could make out no sign of movement close to the low-roofed buildings, but far off, in the distance, beyond the entrance to the valley, there was a faint cloud of dust, no bigger than a man's hand, indicating a group of riders pulling away as fast as their horses would carry them. He brought down his spurs sharply, a little sorry for the horse as he did so, but knowing he would have to hurry. The horse leapt forward then settled down into a tired, dispirited run, hoofs striking hard, metallic echoes from the rocks underfoot.

Jeff rode swiftly down to the floor of the valley, approached the two buildings which stood within a hundred yards of each other. As he drew nearer he noticed the neat way in which everything had been arranged, the plots of tilled earth in an orderly fashion with corn and alfalfa growing sturdily, fresh shiny wire around each square of ground and a pathway leading up to the houses. There were a few hens running round in the dusty courtyards and off at the rear, he saw a handful of cows and a few goats. Squatters, he thought inwardly. He himself was not possessed of this anger towards these people such as the ranchers felt.

It was his belief that the range was free and if a man obtained a Government grant to build on land, then he had a right to be left alone to get on with it. The ranch owners, on the other hand, maintained that they had been there first, that the wire fences injured their cattle, prevented them from free access to the water they had been using for years. Sooner or later, both sides would have to get together to iron out their differences, but until that happened, there would always be bloodshed between the two groups.

He approached the nearer of the two buildings slowly, cautiously, knowing that whoever might be inside would be still trigger-happy after what had happened, would be more inclined to shoot first and then stop to ask questions afterwards. Deliberately, he kept his hands well clear of his holsters, sitting tall and easy in the saddle.

He was less than fifty yards from the front door when a dog started barking at the side of the place and less than five seconds later, a voice from behind one of the windows said harshly, 'That's far enough, mister. Another step and I aim to drop you, whether you make a move for your gun or not.'

'Now hold on a minute,' Jeff called loudly. 'I heard the shootin' while I was in the trees up yonder on top of the hill and rode down to see if there was anythin' I could do to help. I don't mean you folk any harm.'

'No? I figure that you're one of Marsden's bunch, ridin' back to see if any of us are still alive.'

'Marsden?'

'You heard me. Turn your horse and ride on out of here. That way, we'll be sure of you. I'll give you ten seconds and if you ain't out of sight by then, I swear I'll put lead into your back.'

By now, Jeff's gaze had fixed on the smashed window off to one side of the door and he could just make out the faint glint of sunlight glancing off the rifle barrel thrusting out from it and the pale blur of a man's face at the back of the gun. He did not doubt that the other would do exactly as he said and he was on the point of obeying, pulling on the reins to move out, telling himself that this was really no business of his, when a woman's voice called quickly:

'He's not one of Marsden's killers, Father. He could be telling the truth.'

'I don't aim to take that chance,' snapped the other. The gun barrel did not waver.

Jeff could visualise the other increasing his finger pressure on the trigger. He said quickly: 'You're makin' a big mistake. I've got nothin' to do with these men. If I had, do

31

you think I'd ride back like this and risk gettin' a bullet for my trouble?'

There was a long pause as silence settled. Then, slowly, he saw the rifle barrel lower and then be withdrawn. 'All right. Come on in, but keep your hands right where I can see 'em.'

Raising his hands a little, Jeff rode into the dusty courtyard, brought his horse to a standstill in front of the door which opened a few moments later. The man stepped out, the rifle held loosely in his hand. A short, pointed beard covered the lower half of his lean, brown-tanned features. He had pale blue eyes which were still highly suspicious, and a thin streak of a mouth, lips pressed tightly together as he lifted his head and surveyed Jeff for a long moment without speaking.

Finally, he nodded as if satisfied. 'Better light down, mister,' he said, his tone only just genial. 'There's water around the side and you can put your horse over by the fence yonder. He won't stray from there.'

'Thanks.' Jeff nodded briefly, led his horse over to the fence, noticing how new the copper wire was, guessing that these people could not have been here very long. They had probably ridden in last fall, he decided, and this was their first year in the territory. Judging from the corn and alfalfa, they had had a pretty good year, but with this trouble from the big ranchers in the neighbourhood, things could turn out bad for them.

Going back to the house he saw, for the first time, the girl who had stepped out into the courtyard, now standing beside her father. She was tall and willowy, with a strange grace about her that showed in every lovely line of her body. Her gaze was fixed on him as he walked forward, a blend of curiosity and frank challenge. He felt a little uneasy under that direct scrutiny and was a little glad when the man said: 'Better go inside, daughter and set a place for our guest.'

When the girl had gone inside, Jeff said quietly: 'That shootin' I heard while I was in the hills yonder. Trouble from the cattlemen?'

The other's shrewd gaze sharpened at his words. 'How'd you figure that?' he asked, a faint flaring of suspicion visible in his eyes.

'It wasn't difficult.' Jeff grinned slightly. 'Whenever I come across a homestead like this, right in the middle of a cattle range, I can expect trouble, sooner or later. It was no surprise to me.' He paused, then went on, his tone more serious. 'It was cattlemen, wasn't it?'

'That's right. They've been warnin' us to get off the range ever since we got here. Until now all they've done is make threats. But this time, it was somethin' different. They sent out their hired killers to put an end to it, once and for all. Reckon if they'd stayed for a while longer and put in another attack, we'd really have been finished. We couldn't have held out much longer.'

'You got any idea who might be behind it?'

The other's lips curled into a snarling grin. 'Sure. I know.' The other's lids crept nearer, accentuating the bright glint in his eyes. 'Clint Marsden has been threatenin' to drive us out of here if we didn't pull out of our own accord. Ben Landis who brings in supplies for us from the railhead at Culver Creek was killed a couple of weeks ago and his wagon found at the bottom of the gully. The sheriff reckoned that he'd been drunk and gone over the side of the trail, but we know better. They took his body back to town and had it buried real quick, wouldn't let any of us homesteaders take a look at it, but the undertaker let it slip a couple of days ago that old Ben died with a bullet in his back, that he was dead before the wagon went over the edge.'

'So you figure he was murdered?'

The other gave him a bright-sharp stare. 'That's right. Maybe it was meant as a warnin' to the rest of us. Maybe he'd found out a little too much of what was goin' on in town.'

'What sort of things?'

'Hard to say. The way we figure it, Sheriff Parker is in cahoots with the Marsden bunch. We all know that he's elected by the cattlemen. They have the biggest say in the runnin' of the town and Marsden's the biggest of them all. Either Parker does as he's told, or he won't last long as town sheriff.'

'So Marsden is the real law hereabouts?'

The other nodded. 'You're catchin' on real fast,' he said. Whether his tone was approving or not was difficult to tell, but there was a little more respect in his face as he gave Jeff a quick look. He motioned in the direction of the house. 'Better come on inside, mister. Reckon the meal should be about ready.'

Jeff fell into step beside the other. 'The name is Jeff Denver,' he said as he strode forward.

The other nodded his head. 'Mine's Hal Fenner. That was my daughter Susan you met a little while ago. We came out here after her mother died, hoped to make a go of it. Seems that we won't have much chance to do that, although I mean to stay here until I'm run off. I don't intend to back down for men such as Marsden.'

'You seem to have given them somethin' to think about,' Jeff muttered. 'They were hightailin' it out over the valley yonder when I rode up. Figured there must've been about a dozen of 'em. How'd you manage to fight 'em off; just the two of you?'

'You're forgettin' about my neighbours, Clint Shedden and his family yonder,' explained Fenner, jerking a thumb in the direction of the other house. 'Clint has five sons and they're all handy with a gun. Marsden's bunch rode into a crossfire when they tried to shoot it out with us. Guess they figured they'd better pull out and come back another time. Trouble is that if they do return, they'll be ready for us the next time.'

He led the way into the house, showing Jeff into the small parlour. There were plates and eating utensils laid out on the table and the appetising smell of food cooking from the kitchen which opened off the room.

When they were seated around the table, Fenner said to the girl: 'I've been tellin' Mister Denver here about our troubles. It's only a question of time before the same thing which happened to Ben happens to us.'

'What right have they got to drive us off our land?' burst out the girl harshly. 'We bought this ground, got a Government deed for it.'

Jeff shook his head slowly. 'I'm afraid that these men don't see things that way. They maintain that they've been here so long that all of this land belongs to them, that they've been runnin' their cattle on it for more years than they can remember and they don't mean any Government officials in Washington to tell them how to run their business. Not only that, but Washington is a long way from here, and the law has difficulty reachin' out this far. Men like this rancher Marsden are able to run the law themselves. They put men into the office of sheriff who obey whatever they say, bring in hired killers who'll sell their guns to the highest bidder.'

'So you think we ought to give in and leave our home?' For a second, he detected naked scorn in her voice and her eyes were hard as she fixed her gaze on him.

'I didn't say that. All I'm pointin' out is that these men have all of the advantages and you have none. They can bring in more men than you can possibly deal with, overrun your homes and farms, burn your buildings, run off any cattle you've got, kill anybody you hire to help you. And there's nobody will lift a finger to stop 'em. The law – real law and order, just hasn't got to the frontier yet. Maybe it will some day, but how far off that is, I wouldn't know.'

He saw her chin lift a little, wondered why it was that women like her were so beautiful when they were angry. 'We don't scare as easily as that, Mister Denver. If Marsden and the others want a fight on their hands, then they can have one.'

Her glance ran over his face and a faint flicker of expression came to her features, then was gone. She looked at him intently. 'You don't seem to be the usual kind of brush-jumper who rides through here. Do you have some business in Culver Creek?'

He smiled faintly for a moment. Then he shrugged. 'You might call it that,' he answered.

Her glance turned speculative and he was aware of her father eyeing him intently too from across the table. He bent his head to drink the hot coffee and did not look up at them until he had drained the cup.

'You're ridin' into town to kill someone, aren't you?' asked Susan Fenner in a small tight voice, a few moments later.

'Now daughter, you've got no call to say that,' broke in the older man sharply.

'But it's true, isn't it?' she persisted, almost as though she had not heard his words.

Jeff hesitated for a moment and then nodded. 'Yes, it's quite true,' he said finally. 'Not one man, but three.'

She studied him over a thoughtful interval. He had half expected to see a look of horror on her face, but there was nothing like that. Her lips lay close together and her eyes were a little wider than usual. 'What did they do, these three men?' she asked.

He shrugged. 'Enough for me to want to kill them,' he said softly. 'I've been trailin' them for months now. I raised their scent on the other side of the Flats and but for the storm, I'd have been here two or three days ago. But their trail must've got a mite cold by now, and worse than that, they'll have had time to split up or prepare a trap for me.'

'How do you know that they aren't still running?' she asked coolly.

'I don't. But I know these men and if they figure that they have just me to deal with, they'll know that they won't have a better opportunity of killin' me than this. They'll take every advantage of it they can.'

'We've seen nobody ride through this way durin' the past two or three weeks,' said Fenner. He rolled a cigarette, thrust it between his lips and sat back in his chair, easing his back and shoulders into a more comfortable position. 'You're sure they'll be headed for Culver Creek?'

'I'm not really sure of anythin',' Jeff confessed. 'But if that's the only town in these parts then I reckon that's where they'll have gone.'

'Have you considered that they may have thrown in with one of the big outfits hereabouts?' went on the other, blowing smoke into the air. 'That way, they could drop out of sight, yet still keep a watch on you when you ride into town. They'd also have the protection afforded them by the outfit.'

Jeff sat back, thinking that over. There was a lot of truth in what the other said. These cattle outfits tended to become tied together into tight little communities, owing a strange loyalty to the boss. When a man signed on to work with one of them, he had an unwritten right to expect the rest of the men to stand by him against any outsiders. This peculiar bond which held these men together was one of the characteristics of men who rode herd for the big outfits.

He sat quite still over a long interval. Presently, he said: 'I guess you could be right. You know if any of the outfits are hirin' men?'

'Are they handy men with a gun?'

'Yes.'

'Then my guess is that Marsden has signed them on to his payroll. He's always lookin' for men who can be fast with a gun and have no compunction about killin'.'

Jeff rubbed a forefinger down the side of his face. 'If that's so, then I guess it puts me on your side.' He found that most of his tiredness had diminished under the stimulus of the hot coffee. Lighting up a cigarette, he inhaled, while Susan Fenner cleared the meal dishes from the table and carried them through into the kitchen.

Hal Fenner's steady gaze brightened a little; turning sharp and appraising. He shifted slightly in his chair. 'If you're thinkin' of ridin' into Culver Creek and startin' askin' questions around town, you'd best watch your step. A man who rides into town is watched closely by everybody. Pretty soon, word gets back to Marsden and the others and if they reckon he's gettin' too nosy and anxious for information, then they do somethin' about it. A stranger rode in a few months back. There were some who figured he was a Texas Ranger. They found his body out in the Flats after he'd been missin' for a little over a week. Some reckon that it was the buzzard who'd made such a mess of his face so that he was barely recognisable, but there are those who think that a shotgun blast fired from only a few feet away, would have done the same thing. Doesn't seem to matter really which it was. He was dead when they found him and there were tracks in the dust close by, made by half a dozen horses.'

'From what you say, I guess that Culver Creek must be a real hell town, even for this part of the territory.'

'Just remember that and you may stay alive,' agreed the other. He let his glance fall to the guns strapped to Jeff's waist. 'You know how to use those?'

'I can handle them if I have to,' Jeff said modestly.

'I sure hope so. You start goin' after these three men you want, and if they are signed up with Marsden, the rest of that goddamned crew will be after you like the Grim Reaper himself. Your chances of gettin' away from town in one piece won't be good.'

Jeff's eyes widened a little. 'So that's the way of it?' he murmured. He stared down at the glowing tip of the cigarette held between his fingers, the blue spiral of smoke curling up to the ceiling.

'And the man you really have to watch out for is Ed Cranshield, the Triple Bar foreman. Don't be taken in by the way he acts. He tries to make folk think he's the real timid kind. But he's a professional gunman. Marsden wouldn't have hired him for that job if he wasn't. They reckon he's the fastest in the country. I've seen him draw and I doubt if there's a man who can match him, let alone beat him to the draw. He came out with Marsden fifteen years or so ago. The two of them started the Triple Bar ranch with a couple of hundred head of cattle and built it up into what it is now, the biggest for close on a thousand miles. Marsden was the brains behind the outfit, but it was Cranshield who backed up his play with his gun. He took in the gunslingers, killers and gamblers and shaped them into the Triple Bar outfit.'

'I'll keep my eyes open for him,' Jeff nodded. He poured himself a second cup of coffee, then picked it up and walked over to the window, staring out into the sunlight. This was, undoubtedly, one of the reasons why men died every day out here in the west, died in the middle of a dusty street in a frontier town, simply because they were content to believe in the way a man looked and behaved, not thinking that he could be as quick and as cunning as a snake, not knowing how deadly a man might be until it was too late. A faint smile curled the corners of his lips. In his case, there was a slight difference now. He had been forewarned and he could make sure that he never made a mistake which he would not have lived to rectify.

Finishing the coffee, he put the empty cup back on to the table just as Susan Fenner came in from the kitchen. She eyed him for a moment in mild surprise. 'Are you leaving already, Mister Denver?' she asked.

He said, very slowly: 'Much as I'd like to take advantage of your hospitality and the excellent cooking, I have to ride on into town. If I delay too long I might lose their trail and the storm delayed me longer than I'd reckoned on.'

'Will you be coming back this way?'

'I'll see you in a day or two if I may,' he nodded. 'Once I know what has happened to these men, I can lay my plans accordingly.'

'If they are joined up with Marsden's outfit, you won't be able to fight them all,' said the older man, scraping back his chair and getting up from the table. 'We'd help if we could, but there are only a few of us at the moment and even though there are more homesteaders movin' out west all the time, it's sure as God made little apples, that Marsden means to finish us before more can get here to back us.'

Jeff made to say something, but remained silent. He could see that depression obviously chilled the other's spirit, that in spite of the fact that the attack of that day had been beaten off without any casualties on their side, the worst was yet to come and this had been only the preliminary skirmish of the real battle.

As he rode out half an hour later, he noticed the men working in the plot around the other homestead, guessed that these were Clint Shedden and his sons. They watched him closely as he rode by, but there were no expressions on their faces and it was impossible to tell what they were thinking.

The late afternoon sunlight filtered down through the leaves of the tall pines which stood on either side of the trail, turned green by the time it reached the ground. The air here was cool and filled with the sharply aromatic tang of the trees and the ground underfoot was thick with pine needles which had fallen over the years, forming a dense carpet that muffled the sound of the horse's hooves.

Crossing a bare patch, he reached more timber, climbing now. He rode like a man pressed for time, his mind drawing back into his thoughts. An hour onward, he came to a narrow bridge which spanned a wide river and somewhere close by there was a waterfall whose racket was clearly audible as it plummeted down the side of the hill, the mist of its spray lifting damply into the air about him.

He rode into Culver Creek, from the north-east, arriving there before full darkness, but after the sun had gone down and the shadows were lying huge and thick in the streets. His first impression was one of sprawling ugliness. There seemed to have been few plans made when Culver Creek had been started. The main street ran a little off centre from one edge of the town to the other, little more than a wide track, some thirty yards across, dusty now during the dry season, but once the rains came it would be a river of mud, literally several inches deep.

On either side of the street which glimmered faintly in the last vestiges of daylight like a main artery running through the town, the houses and stores lay in a vast, irregular grouping without rhyme or reason as to their layout. To Jeff's keen eye, it looked as though the place had just been thrown together by a handful of men, building another store, another saloon whenever they figured they needed one, and putting it any place where there was land available for them to build. It held the oddest assortment of places he had ever seen. The bank, one of the few really imposing structures in town was adjacent to a low-roofed store that looked as if it was the original building in Culver Creek and directly opposite was a feed merchant's shop, the dusty window gleaming dully in the faint light.

As he rode, keeping into the dead centre of the street, his eyes wary and watchful, he felt a little of the tension seeping into his bones. It was a feel he had experienced before on several occasions, one he had learned from past experience never to ignore. The old ways of violence which had been rife in the days before the war, were still here; maybe they were now under the surface where they were less easily seen, but they were there, just the same.

He rode with his shoulders hunched forward a little, then tried to force himself to relax, reminding himself that the flesh of his shoulders was no barrier to a bullet anyway. The little itch between his shoulder blades was slowly increasing in intensity.

Yellow beams of light were already beginning to show through open windows and doors, casting patches of light and shadow over the slatted boardwalks and he glimpsed the shadows of men standing or seated under the wooden overhangs which hid their features from his view, giving him only the impression of huddled blobs of shadows stretched out at intervals along either side.

A little over halfway along the street, another road, not quite as wide as that along which he rode, wound away to the west, its further end lost in the encroaching darkness. He gave it a swift, all-embracing glance, then looked ahead of him and spotted the livery stables set a little further back from the street than the stores and buildings on either side. Heading his mount towards them, he dismounted at the tie-rail, walked his horse into the dark gloom of the stables. A man drifted out from the back, a dimly-seen shadow, the face occasionally highlighted by the glowing end of the cigarette between his lips, a red glow thrown over his mouth and high-bridged nose whenever he inhaled.

The groom came right up to Jeff, peered closely at him, eyes bright in the shadow of his face, then jerked a thumb over his shoulder. 'You'll find a stall empty back there.'

Jeff led the horse into one of the empty stalls, settled it down and then walked back.

'You reckon on stayin' in town long?' inquired the

groom. He stood with his back against one of the wooden uprights, eyes roaming over Jeff's tall, spare figure.

'Depends on how long it takes me to finish some business here.'

The other murmured something under his breath, then dropped the glowing butt of his cigarette into the dust and ground it out with his heel. Looking up, he said: 'The charge is a dollar a night for the horse, includin' food and water.'

Jeff dug into his pocket, brought out a couple of dollars and handed them to the other. 'If I have to stay here any longer I'll give you more,' he told the groom.

'Sure.' The other nodded his head quickly, thrust the coins into his shirt with a rapid movement of his hand. He glanced up and down the street as if anxious not to be seen, then said in a low tone. 'You want some advice, mister?'

'What sort of advice?' Jeff asked.

'Good advice. The sort that might stop you from bein' killed. Stay the night at the hotel and at first light tomorrow mornin' pick up your mount and ride on out of here, head east or west, but keep ridin' until you're miles away from Culver Creek and don't come back.'

Jeff looked at him suspiciously. 'Why give me a warnin' like that?'

The groom was silent for a long moment, then he lowered his tone a little more, his voice barely above a whisper. 'Because three men rode into town four days ago. They put up their mounts here the first night. Next day they came for them. They was with Ed Cranshield, seemed on right friendly terms with him. He's the foreman of Marsden's spread, the Triple Bar. I hear they're now signed on the payroll, but they were askin' around town yesterday about some *hombre* who might come ridin' in, who might start askin' questions.' The other's brows went up a little. 'Could be that you're the *hombre* they're lookin' for. If you

43

are, then your chances of ridin' out from here a couple of days from now are pretty slender.'

CHAPTER 3

GUNSMOKE WARNING

Jeff caught the odour of food as he entered the narrow lobby of the hotel and walked over to the desk. The pimply-faced clerk placed the register in front of him, waited until he had signed it, then spun the book back into position, glancing down at the name he had written there. Then he turned and took down a key from the rack on the wall, handed it over.

'You can get a bite of supper in the dining-room yonder in ten minutes, Mister Denver,' he said, pointing.

'And a bath?' Jeff asked.

'Certainly. I'll get the swamper to draw some hot water for you, but it'll take the best part of half an hour. Would you like to get something to eat first?'

'All right.' Jeff nodded, took the key and walked up the creaking stairs, along the passage at the top, finding his room halfway along. It faced down on to the street and without putting on the light he walked over to the window and glanced out into the dimly-lit street immediately below him. There were few men about, this being supper time when things were normally slacker than usual. A rider came in front of the saloon opposite, hitched his mount to the rail and went inside, pushing open the doors with the flat of his hands, his face briefly illuminated by the strong yellow light that spilled from the place. The tinny sound of a piano reached Jeff's ears and there was the lilting sound of a woman singing, a melodious blend of notes that touched a half-forgotten chord in his mind and made him think for a moment of days long past, before the war, before this journey of vengeance and hate which he had been forced to undertake.

Wearily, he turned back from the window, dropped his saddle roll on to the floor and went out, locking the door behind him. There were several people in the dining-room when he went inside but he managed to find himself a table some distance from the door and sat with his shoulders against the wall, looking about him as he waited for his meal. There was a deep-seated weariness in him and he had to deliberately force his body to relax, the taut muscles to loosen.

He ate slowly when the meal came, savouring the food which was far better cooked than he had anticipated. When he had finished, he pushed the empty plate away from him and drew the cup of coffee towards him, his fingers curved around it absently, as he glanced about him.

A man came into the room, paused just inside the doorway and stared about him, before fixing his eyes on Jeff. As the other came towards him across the whole length of the room, Jeff caught the brief twinkle of the light on the badge which the man wore. He eyed him thoughtfully, making up his mind about the other in the short space of time it took the sheriff to walk to his table.

The other stood near the chair opposite for a long moment staring down at him out of suspicious eyes, the lids drawn close together in a tight, straight line. Finally, he cleared his throat noisily and said: 'You the *hombre* who just rode into town, mister?'

Jeff fixed a hard stare on the other, then gave a curt nod. 'That's right, Sheriff,' he said quietly. 'And you're Parker.'

For a second, a tiny gust of expression drifted over the other's bluff, red-veined features, but it was gone almost before it could be seen. He pulled the chair back and lowered himself into it without being asked, placed his elbows on the table in front of him and rested his weight on them. Jeff judged that the other was flabby underneath, that he had allowed himself to go to fat, and in a lawman, particularly in a frontier town such as this, that could be a dangerous mistake. A man had to be fast with a gun and quick on his feet if he was to uphold the law in these parts.

'You got somethin' on your mind, Sheriff?'

'Very likely,' muttered the other, 'and most of it concerns you.'

'Don't see why,' Jeff answered innocently. He took out the makings of a cigarette and deliberately rolled the tobacco in the strip of brown paper, licking it and placing it between his lips in movements which could have been construed as insolent.

For a moment, he saw the anger deep within the other man in the tightening of his fingers where they were laced together, in the set of his mouth and jaw. The anger stayed for a long moment, then dissipated as he let it fade. His features grew faintly amused.

'You sound like another of these cocky gunfighters who drift into Culver Creek and then move out again, or we pick 'em up in the middle of the street and take 'em up to Boot Hill and give them a permanent spot in town. You look too like a man who lives by the gun.'

'If there's any trouble, I try to avoid it if I can, but if it comes lookin' for me then I don't back out of it.'

Evidently Sheriff Parker saw nothing good in this outlook and said so. 'When a fella rides into my town after visitin' those squatters out in the valley, then I can only assume that he's lookin' for trouble. This is a cattlemen's town and we don't want nesters, or nester-lovers here. You got that clear?'

'Seems to me this town is a mite jumpy,' Jeff said. 'From what I've heard, there's big trouble ready to flare up at any minute and when it does, you're likely to be right in the middle of it.'

'Just what is that supposed to mean?' demanded the other harshly. 'You been listenin' to the lies those squatters have been tellin' you?'

Jeff shrugged and pursed his lips. 'I listen to everybody's side of the story,' he told the sheriff. 'And then I make up my own mind as to who's tellin' the truth and who's lyin'.'

Parker's gaze hardened just a shade. He did not seem to have been expecting this answer and for a moment he was bewildered and nonplussed. Then he snapped: 'I don't particularly care what your idea is about all this. I'm responsible for keepin' law and order here in Culver Creek. I intend to do that and if you step out of line just once, I'll have you inside the jail so fast you won't know what's hit you.'

Jeff sat back in his chair, checked an inclination to get up and walk away from the other. He continued to study Parker. There was something about this man which didn't quite fit in with what he had been told by Fenner, something that meant trouble. Something really arrogantly dangerous too. He could feel his own angry hardness rising within him, reaching out and touching the same kind of hardness that came from Parker.

'I'll think over what you've said, Sheriff,' he muttered, draining his coffee.

Parker snapped: 'You won't have much time to think

about it if Marsden rides into town. If he gets to hear that you've been sidin' with those troublemakers in the valley, your life won't be worth a bent nickel.'

Jeff grinned at that, his lips twisted into a smile which was faintly vicious. 'I've learned how to take care of myself the hard way,' he told the other, 'and if Marsden or any of his bunch of hired killers want to make any trouble then they've come to the right place for it if they decide to tangle with me.'

Parker sat quite still for several seconds, staring at him, eyes narrowed down to mere slits. Then he got to his feet, leaned forward with his face close to Jeff's for a moment before saying tightly: 'Don't try to buck Marsden and the Triple Bar crew if you know what's good for you. They're real dynamite. And he's signed up three more fast men with their guns. This ain't a threat, just a friendly warnin'.'

'Like I said, I'll consider it,' Jeff said. He sat forward and watched as the other walked away. Inside the doorway, the sheriff turned and threw a swift, enigmatic glance back at him as if he were wondering just what sort of man he was, a reckless fool or one of those real killers from down south, along the Texas border. Then he swung away and vanished along the lobby.

Jeff had just finished his smoke when the clerk came in and sidled over to the table. 'Your bath's ready any time you want it, Mister Denver,' he said ingratiatingly.

'Thanks.' Jeff followed him to the small room at the back of the hotel. The bath was, in reality, a long metal basin, perhaps seven feet in length, and although it lacked some of the usual comforts, the water was hot and as he lay in it, letting it soak into every pore of his body, he felt the tightness drain from him, utterly soothing and relaxing.

He lay for the best part of half an hour before climbing out and towelling himself dry, rubbing his skin briskly. It was the first time he had felt really clean for as long as he could remember.

Going back up to his room, he put on a clean shirt, dressed, and went down into the lobby. The clerk put down the newspaper he was reading as Jeff went over.

'Which is the best saloon in this town?' he asked.

'The Broken Bow,' answered the other quickly. 'It's down the street about two hundred yards on the other side.'

'That the one where Marsden and the Triple Bar crew usually drink when they're in town?'

'I think so, Mister Denver.' There was a speculative look in the clerk's eyes. 'You goin' to sign on for that bunch?'

Jeff grinned. 'Somehow, I've got the feelin' that Marsden won't want to sign me on his payroll,' he said thinly.

He went out into the street, sniffing the cold, clear air that sighed between the rows of buildings, funnelled by the main street. The sky was dark but clear and the brilliant stars seemed to have moved down to the earth and become entangled along the roofs of the buildings. All around him as he stepped down off the boardwalk, there was movement and talk. A few riders swung in from the darkened, narrow alleys which branched off the main street, stretching away to the outskirts of town. Their faces were caught at irregular intervals by the beams of lights which cut shining swathes through the darkness of the street. Along the street a piece, he caught sight of a bunch of men standing outside the Broken Bow saloon. He watched them idly as he made his way forward and then with a growing alertness and concern as he fell to wondering if any of the three men he was hunting might be there, among them. Several of the men gave him a quick glance as he walked past them, up the wooden steps and through the swinging doors. Their glances were brief enough, but Jeff was not fooled by them. All of these men had eyed him closely, seeking in their minds and memories for some fleeting picture of him, trying to recall if his face was familiar, trying to place him into some particular niche in their minds.

Approaching the bar, Jeff flagged his head at one of the two bartenders, rested his elbows in front of him as the man sidled forward.

'Sour mash,' he said quietly.

When the drink came, he curled his hand tightly around the bottle and held on to it until the bartender shrugged and moved sway, but the other continued to give him quick stares of suspicion from the far end of the bar and once he went over to speak to the other bartender and both men eyed him covertly. Then the second man moved away and went through a door at the back of the counter. He came out a few moments later, gave his companion a quick nod and then went on with his work.

Evidently he had been through to tell the owner of the saloon that a stranger had walked in and was standing at the bar. This was surely one hell of a town, Jeff reflected, as he drank quietly, watching what went on at his back through the crystal mirror behind the bar.

Several minutes passed and then the far door opened and a man stepped out. He was dressed in rich brocade, a silk shirt with frilled cuffs and neck and a diamond tie-pin that glinted every colour imaginable as he came forward. He stopped a couple of feet from Jeff, eyed him from the corner of his vision for some time, evidently trying to sum him up before speaking. There was something clearly balanced in his mind and he finally decided to put it into words.

'You're not with the Triple Bar outfit are you, mister?'

'I just rode into town this evening,' Jeff said. He sipped the whisky. 'I'm not lined up with anybody.'

'Not even lookin' for a job with one of the ranch outfits?' There was a note of insistent query in the other's voice.

'No. Should I be?'

'Sometimes it can be dangerous to stay in the middle. A man is twice as likely to be hit by a bullet.'

'It could be that I don't intend to stick around long enough for that to happen.'

The other's smile was amused, leaving the twinkle in his eyes a little. 'Even a day can be too long in Culver Creek.'

'You mean that if Marsden discovers somebody is in town who doesn't want to join up with him, he may decide to do somethin' about it?'

'That's exactly what I did mean,' agreed the other. 'They don't usually ride into town on a Thursday night. But one or two of them might just drop in and they could start trouble.'

Jeff gave the other's words prolonged study. Somehow, he figured, word of his stopping by the Fenner place had gone ahead of him into Culver Creek. How it had travelled so swiftly he did not know; but bad news always did and he realised, for the first time, that his position might be even more precarious than he had thought so far.

He finished his drink, stood in thoughtful silence for a moment, then reached for the bottle and poured a second glassful. He eyed the other over the rim of the glass as he lifted it.

'You own this saloon?' he asked, more to make conversation than to get an answer to his question.

'That's right,' acknowledged the other. 'I came here when the town was first started some twenty years ago. This was the first saloon we built.'

'Business good?'

'Sort of. I get the Triple Bar crew in now and again, but this ain't a big town.'

Jeff nodded. He made a cigarette, lit it and drew in the sweet-smelling smoke, let it out slowly through his nostrils. He had the feeling that this man was worried, although trying not to show it outwardly. For a moment, the other's

52

gaze flicked over Jeff's shoulder in the direction of the door. The look quickened Jeff's interest and the faint draught of cool air on the back of his neck was a warning he could not ignore. Lifting his glance swiftly, he stared into the mirror behind the fat man, saw that two men had entered the saloon, had paused to stare about them for a moment before moving forward. Just as their gaze lighted on his back, he saw the quick look that passed between them. Then they sauntered forward, arms swinging loosely by their sides.

The saloon owner said out of the corner of his mouth, his tone low, not moving his lips as he spoke. 'This may mean trouble for you, mister. Steer clear of it if you can.'

Jeff smiled grimly at the other's discomfiture. For a moment there was a strange sense of restlessness in him, even though he had never seen either of these two men before. One was a big man with sharp grey eyes and a high-bridged nose, his mouth a long thin gash across his features. He was quite obviously a cowman, Jeff decided, short, wiry, lean-hipped, his eyes the palest blue that Jeff had ever seen. They never seemed to remain watching anything for any length of time but were always moving searching out faint movements in the corners of the room. A nervous man, he figured, yet that did not quite fit in with the guns he wore slung low at his hips, their butts worn smooth from long use.

They came up to the bar, stood against it a few feet from where Jeff stood. For several minutes the silence in the saloon built up. Jeff noticed that several of the blackjack players at the tables had stopped their game and were watching the scene at the bar. *Something is going to break loose pretty soon,* he reflected grimly; *and he was likely to find himself in the middle of it whether he liked it or not.*

'You got some reason for bein' in town or are you just drifting through, mister?' asked the big man suddenly, still not looking round at Jeff, apparently addressing no one in particular.

Jeff turned slowly, propping himself against the bar on one elbow. His look was deliberately insolent as he stared at the other. He flicked the second man a short glance, then drawled, 'If you're talkin' to me, friend, I'd say that was my business and nobody else's.'

This time the other did turn, giving Jeff a prolonged study, his eyes thoughtful. The remark, nor the tone, did not seem to have aroused any anger in him, unless it was there, but too deep and under too tight a control to show. The remark seemed to have interested him rather than evoked any anger and this was a reaction which Jeff had not expected; for this reason, he watched the other a little more closely. He eyed the big man's face steadily, looking for any sign of change there.

'You seem to be very sure of yourself,' said the other after a pause. 'I'd say off-hand that you're here lookin' for somebody, ready for trouble. If you are, then I don't like it.'

Jeff raised his brows a little, feeling the sudden surge of anger tighten the muscles of his chest. He clenched his teeth a little, said tautly: 'Makes no difference to me whether you like it or not.' He pushed himself away from the bar. 'Let me give you a little piece of advice. Don't make statements like that when you're standin' in front of me. If you want to make somethin' out of this, then put in your chips right now.'

Out of the corner of his eye, he saw the short man move a pace away from the bar, standing so that both of his hands were free-moving. His eyes had narrowed down a little, were now fixed on Jeff's face like those of a snake, empty and devoid of any feeling.

For an instant, he thought the other meant to make a reach for his gun, then the big man said sharply. 'No, Ed. This *hombre* has to be taught a lesson he won't forget.' The other unbuckled his gunbelt, let it drop to the floor in front of the bar, then took off his jacket. There was no mistaking his intention now.

'You'd better back off, mister,' Jeff said harshly. 'I don't want to have to fight you, especially since I don't know what all this is about.'

'My name is Marsden,' said the big man, his voice very quiet, soft. 'I own this place, lock, stock and barrel. I give the orders around here and if I say that a man gets out of town, then he goes. But first, I make sure that he forgets any ideas he may have of ridin' back this way again. Now drop that gunbelt.'

Jeff hesitated for a moment. The other looked rough and strong and there was also something about him which suggested he was a dirty fighter who knew all of the tricks of infighting and would not hesitate to apply them. But it was not this which made Jeff pause. He said slowly, through his teeth, 'I don't fight anybody when there are guns on me.' He jerked his head in the direction of Ed who had moved a little further from the bar, his hands swinging loose near his gunbutts.

Marsden growled out a fierce oath. 'Never mind about Ed. He won't sit in on this little play.' Without turning his head or taking his fierce glance from Jeff's face, he said: 'Don't interfere in this, Ed.'

The other relaxed, moved back to the bar and stood with his elbows resting on it. The saloon had grown very quiet, the tension now building up almost to explosion point. Very slowly, Jeff shucked his gunbelt, let it fall to the floor. Scarcely had he done so, than the other came charging forward, his head lowered, his arms reaching out to get Jeff around the waist and bear him backward into one of the tables.

There was now no alternative for Jeff. The other was committed and there was the fierce, hard shine of battle in his eyes, the hunger for combat written all over his flushed features. Plainly the other considered himself to be a past master in the art of rough-and-tumble, but he was not prepared for Jeff as the other side-stepped, waited calmly until Marsden was up to him and then swung a short, jabbing right which caught the cattleman flush on the side of the face, staggering him as he fell forward off balance.

Marsden recovered himself quickly, swung and sent two blows towards Jeff's face. He slid under the first, blocking off most of the sting with his raised arm, but the second struck him on the cheek and he felt the fire down the side of his face, then a numbness which was even worse than the pain.

Before he could brace himself, Marsden swung again. Jeff did not see the other's tightly-bunched fist until it was less than an inch from his mouth. Then it was too late, he reeled backward, his shoulders hitting the edge of the bar. Desperately, he allowed himself to slide along it, feeling blood on his lips, tasting it salty between his teeth. People were yelling in the background and he could hear them scrambling out of the way. Through a red haze, he saw Marsden moving in again, his big grin crazy to kill. Keeping his shoulders against the edge of the bar, Jeff rolled again and Marsden smashed head first into the front of the bar. He gave vent to a bull-like roar, staggered back and came around once more, only to meet Jeff's fist in the face. Jeff felt it connect with the other's nose with a remarkably satisfying solidity.

The blow stopped the other in his tracks. For a long second, Marsden fell back, sobbing air down into his lungs, glaring at Jeff through eyes that were now wide open. Jeff was clear and he stood there, waiting, not once looking away from the bigger, heavier man, knowing that the instant he did so, the other would launch himself forward, fingers curled into talons, seeking out his eyes.

The cattleman was rocked. Clearly he had not expected this, had figured on taking Jeff within moments of starting the fight. Now he must have realised that sheer brute strength was not going to win it for him. He would have to use cunning and some of the dirty tricks he had learned from a host of other battles such as this during his career.

He waited, sawed in a deep, shuddering breath, then came forward more slowly this time, planting each foot solidly forward. Jeff waited for him, watchful for every move the other made, trying to out-think and out-guess him. Marsden feinted to the left, then suddenly lunged forward, head lowered. For a moment the move took Jeff by surprise. He had been expecting the other to bring up a short, jabbing right. Instead, there was the solid blow of the other's lowered head socketing into his stomach. It felt as though all of the air had been driven from his lungs by the force of the impact. For a moment, there was a red haze dancing in front of his vision. Shaking his head in an attempt to clear it, he slid further along the bar, caught the other by the shoulders and then swung sharply, bringing the other round with him, so that it was now Marsden who stood with his back against the bar.

Unmindful of the pain which filled his body, gripping his stomach and chest, he swung two sharp blows at the other's head, but Marsden had been waiting for this and the rancher had lowered his head again, curling it into Jeff's shoulder so that the blows glanced off the top of his skull, doing him little damage.

Then Jeff made a mistake. He moved away, but just a shade too slowly. The other had guessed at his intention from what had happened before and he lunged forward, clasping his arms around the small of Jeff's back, locking his fingers at the base of his spine, bearing down on him with all of his weight. Driven backward, Jeff crashed into one of the tables, sending it over on to its side, the chairs around it collapsing into matchwood as the two men fell over them.

Instinct made Jeff twist, even as he fell, and it was his

hip which absorbed the blow which the other's knee had aimed for his groin, a blow which would have put him out of the fight at once if it had connected. With a round-about grip on Jeff's body, Marsden began to apply pressure, squeezing with all of his tremendous strength. Jeff struggled to ease the pain of the bear-like hug, knowing that he would soon have to break that hold or his spine would be snapped like a brittle twig. Gasping air down into his heaving lungs, he fought off the blackness of unconsciousness that came out of the corners of the room to envelop him.

Marsden continued to apply pressure. His grin was now one of triumph and his breath, coming in hard gasps told of the effort he was putting in to kill Jeff. Suddenly, without warning, Jeff relaxed completely, his body going limp in the other's grasp. The manoeuvre took Marsden completely by surprise. His grip around Jeff's body loosened momentarily. It was only for a second or so, but it was enough. At that moment, Jeff whirled free, rolled over twice on the floor and then came up on to his feet, drawing in deep shuddering breaths, forcing himself to think clearly. There was a dull roaring in his brain and he could still feel a trickle of blood oozing down his chin from the corner of his bruised mouth.

Marsden staggered upright, brushed the hair from his eyes, then came lunging forward. He was really angry now, and his anger made him throw all caution to the wind as he moved forward. Jeff rocked forward slightly on the balls of his feet. When Marsden swung all the way from his knees, it was comparatively easy for him to move his head so that the other missed and fell forward. Waiting his opportunity, Jeff swung a sharp chopping blow at the back of the rancher's neck as he fell. The cattleman, hanging on all fours where he had collapsed at Jeff's feet, gave a choked-off grunt of agony, struggled desperately to rise again, almost made it, then slid forward on to his face in

58

the dirt as another merciless blow from the side of Jeff's hand hit him just behind his ear. He lay quite still and did not make another sound.

Bending swiftly, Jeff caught at the unconscious man's shoulders and hauled them off the floor, but not to help the other to his feet. When his hands came out into the open again, one of them held a gun and the blue-shining barrel was pointed directly at Ed's chest as his hand made a swift move towards his gun.

'Just hold it right there, Ed,' Jeff said tautly, 'otherwise I might be tempted to let you have it between the belly and the breastbone.'

Ed froze, eyes blazing with a feral light. Then he lowered his arm slowly and reluctantly as Jeff got to his feet, keeping the gun trained on him.

'I figured a low-down skunk like you would try to plug me in the back the minute you saw how this fight was goin' to end,' he said, grinning fiercely. Looping the gunbelt around his middle, he fastened it with one hand, then lifted his unfinished glass of whisky from the bar, tossed it down in as single gulp and moved towards the doors.

Reaching them, he paused with his back to them, said softly: 'If you still feel lucky, Ed, I'll pouch my gun and give you the benefit of the draw.' He deliberately and coolly thrust the gun back into its holster and stood waiting. When the man at the bar made no move during the next fifteen seconds, Jeff's lips curled into a scornful smile. Turning his back on the other as though his shoulders presented an invulnerable target, he pushed open the doors with the flat of his hand and walked out.

Once on the boardwalk, he moved quickly. There was always the chance that Ed Cranshield, nettled by the remarks which Jeff had made in the saloon, would come out and try to shoot him down without warning. Reaching the end of the block, he paused in the shadows and watched the doors of the saloon.

When they did burst open, it was one of the bartenders who came hurrying out. Glancing up and down the street for a moment, he turned and ran off in the opposite direction to Jeff. When no one else followed him, Jeff hitched his gunbelt a little higher about his waist. Cranshield would probably be waiting for fresh orders from Marsden, rather than come gunning for him on his own initiative.

But he knew that he had to keep moving. He had shown his hand in the saloon and by now, all of Culver Creek would know that he had fallen foul of Marsden, the man who was the law in town, the real power at the back of it. Very soon, once Marsden got back to the Triple Bar ranch, the word would go out and Marsden's remaining men, including perhaps the three he had come here to find, would be out searching, scattering about the town, moving swiftly and with purpose through the night, probably with an incentive of a kind urging them on. Marsden was the kind of man who would never forgive him for beating him up like that in front of those other men in the saloon.

He crossed hurriedly, moved off the main street, through a weed-strewn back lot and into a wealth of dark shadow that lay over the alley near an unkempt building which may have been a store or a church. In the darkness it was impossible for him to tell which.

Not until he had reached the shadows and was moving through them quietly, on padded feet, did he hear the unmistakable sharp snippet of sound which came drifting to him from the distant corner, borne towards him by the faint breeze. It was the sound which anyone, having heard it once before, would never forget or mistake it for anything else; it was the cocking of a gun. He paused where he was for the barest fraction of a second, then dived headlong for the low brick wall. The crashing racket of the gunshot blasted the night apart and sent a multitude of shrieking echoes racing among the abandoned buildings in this part of the town. The slug struck the top of the wall and ricocheted away into the distance with the thin, high-pitched wail of tortured metal and Jeff felt splinters of wood and pieces of stone strike the top of his head and burn his cheek as he thrust his body lower into the dirt.

His own gun was out, balanced perfectly in the palm of his hand and he wriggled swiftly forward, reached the end of the wall and peered cautiously around it, seeking the shape of the hidden gunman. It was obvious that the other, whoever he was, had recognised him, otherwise he would not have fired from cover and without warning.

He could see nothing in the long, huge shadows where the gloom drew down from the tall buildings. Letting his breath go in a long, silent exhalation, he waited, not making a sound, letting the stillness draw out, waiting for the other to break. The dry-gulcher would have guessed that his slug had not found its mark and that he was just waiting for some movement at which to aim.

Jeff did not have too long to wait. The man had no real nerve. Very soon the stillness got on his nerves, ate at them like acid and Jeff heard the sharp intake of breath as the strain told on the other. The sound gave him away. Narrowing his eyes, Jeff peered in the direction of the slight sound and was able to pick out the small hump of shadow off to his right. Even as he fixed his gaze on it, the shadow lifted itself, stood lumped against the background.

Jeff levelled his gun on the shape and tightened his finger on the trigger, taking up the slack. Why not just squeeze off one shot and have it done with right there and then, he thought? But he knew inwardly that it would have to be another way. He watched the shadow move again, with nothing on his face. Then he called sharply: 'Drop that gun! Stand right where you are.'

The other's answer was immediate. Throwing himself down, the gunman loosed off a couple of shots, both of which went wild. Swinging the gun in his hand, Jeff fired swiftly, the sound of gunfire bucketing into the night. He saw the man turn and begin to run, saw the way the other held one of his arms low by his side and guessed that at least one of his bullets had found its mark. But the other was not so badly wounded that he could not run. The sound of running feet was clearly audible in the distance, followed by the harsh scrape as the other thrust his way between upthrusting walls of stone.

The metallic sound of spurs dragging in the dust made it possible for Jeff to follow the other's rapid progress and getting to his feet, he ran forward, came up on to the brick wall that rose directly in front of him, gave a grunt of pain as his arm caught against it, almost tripped over some other invisible obstacle in the blackness, then forced his way through a narrow alley that led into the darkness of the outskirts of the town. He caught a brief glimpse of the other in the distance where the pale light at the far end of the alley showed against the much darker background.

Instinctively he triggered off another shot, heard it whine off the stone wall, knew that it had not hit the running man. A moment later, the other vanished from sight around the end of the alley and Jeff approached it more cautiously, knowing that the other could be lying in wait for him there, waiting to put a bullet into him the instant he showed himself beyond the alley mouth.

He was still half a dozen feet from the end when he caught the racket of a horse being pushed hard. Running the last few feet he burst out of the alley just in time to see the gunman spurring his mount away into the distance. Reluctantly, he lowered his arm, then thrust the gun back into its holster.

He made his way back to the hotel by a circuitous, back-alley route. A late-rising Comanche moon threw a silver, cold light over the town so that the houses and stores on either side stood out in stark silhouette. There seemed to be plenty of action near the middle of the town and he paused and listened to it from outside the hotel, then went into the building, made his way up to his room. Not putting on the light, he undressed slowly, then stood near the window, peering down into the shadow-darkened street. In the eerie moonlight a solitary rider, driving a buckboard, made his way out of town, not hurrying. Jeff followed the other with his gaze until the man had vanished into the darkness which lay on every side of the town.

Going back to the low bed, he stretched himself out on it, feeling the cool touch of the sheets on his tired, bruised body. His mouth had stopped bleeding but his lips were still sore and felt as if they were swollen to twice their normal size. He fingered his cheek where Marsden's ham-like fists had burned their way along the flesh. Wincing, he felt his jaw, wriggling it experimentally from side to side, feeling pain jar through his head.

He would undoubtedly be stiff in the morning from the beating he had received, but there was a solid sense of satisfaction in him as he remembered how he had last seen Marsden, lying unconscious on the floor of the saloon. The other would never get over that.

Turning over on to his side, he thought that he must now be very careful so long as he remained in this territory. Marsden had a great many friends and men he could call upon to do his bidding without asking questions.

CHAPTER 4

VENGEANCE RIDER

Sheriff Block Parker stood outside the livery stables, picking his teeth with a long, pointed toothpick, running his gaze up and down the dusty, sunlit street. The groom sidled out of the building, stood a few feet away and built himself a smoke. After a while, he said: 'You still reckon that *hombre* who rode into town yesterday is hell bent for trouble, Block?'

Parker remained silent for a moment, then stirred himself, let his lids droop lazily over his eyes. Taking off his hat he mopped his sweating brow with his kerchief. Eventually, he said: 'I wish I knew why he was here, Charlie. I've seen plenty of saddlebums come driftin' through town in my time and I can usually put these men into one of two classes: those who come ridin' with the law closin' in on their trail, lookin' for sanctuary and those who come lookin' for trouble. He don't fit into either class.'

'You got any pictures o' him in your office?' queried the other shrewdly.

'Nope.' Parker shook his head. 'I checked on that as soon as I'd had a talk with him in the hotel last night. I also wired Clayton in Gunsight. He's not wanted there either.'

'So?'

'So I figure it this way. He's ridin' after somebody, and if he's not careful, he'll ride foul of Marsden and the Triple Bar bunch.'

The groom glanced at Parker out of the corner of his eye, then sucked the cigarette smoke into his lungs reflectively.

Parker rubbed the palms of his hands down the side of his legs. He had been troubled ever since word had reached him of what had happened in the saloon the previous evening. He had not expected this drifter Denver, to tackle Marsden on the other's ground. That was, in Parker's view, a plumb sure way of committing suicide. Maybe this *hombre* was one of those gunslicks from the Mexico order. He had heard of them. Billy the Kid, Charlie Trevis and others like them. Rash, reckless men who did not care whether they lived or died, men for whom this constant pitting of themselves against others, was the very spice of life. They thought of nothing beyond the danger and the exhilaration. Daily, along the cowtowns of the southern frontier, men were shot dead in saloons and in the wide, dusty streets.

It could be that Jeff Denver was another of them; a man with a deceptive look. He rubbed his chin thoughtfully. Marsden had not yet ridden back into town, but Parker did not doubt that he would soon, possibly bringing his full crew with him. When that happened, all hell would erupt. Marsden was not known for his even temper. He would want to rid himself of this man as soon as possible.

Sighing, he thrust his hat back on his head. There was a raw-looking red mark on his forehead where the sweat band had bitten into his flesh. This was all his own fault, he thought tightly. He had allowed Marsden to talk him into taking this office as sheriff when he had, in reality, no real wish for it. Certainly it had partially satisfied his desire for power, but there had always been that knowledge at the back of his mind that he was nothing more than a puppet, manipulated by Marsden, jumping to every command that the other issued.

Now, the thing which he had been dreading all these years had come to pass. There was real trouble in Culver Creek, trouble so big that he could not handle it himself. But now that it was about to break, he had the inescapable feeling that it was up to him to do something about it. He had tried to warn Denver the previous night of the consequences of trying to buck Marsden, but the trouble had flared in spite of this. He himself had no idea which of the two was to blame, although inwardly he suspected that it had been Marsden. He felt reasonably certain that Denver had not ridden into town to settle a score with the rancher. It was someone else he was trailing, maybe one of those three men who had ridden in a few days earlier and signed up with Marsden. But the rancher could not stand the idea of having anybody in town who would not knuckle under to him. He tried to tell himself that maybe Ed Cranshield would be ordered to take care of Denver and that would be the end of the matter as far as everybody was concerned.

A man stepped out on to the boardwalk opposite and he narrowed his attention on the other, stiffened a little as he saw that it was Jeff Denver. For a moment he stared at the other in surprise. The man was walking down into the street from the hotel as though he didn't have a care in the world, as if nothing had happened in town to warn him of danger. The other did not even seem to care at all for Marsden, or Ed Cranshield.

'You goin' to warn him away, Sheriff?' asked the groom, noticing the direction of the other's glance.

'Guess I'll have to.' Parker started forward, feeling the tension begin to rise within him.

The rage in Marsden had subsided a little that morning.

He had stormed savagely at Ed Cranshield for not having shot it out with Denver that night in the saloon, sneered at him for not accepting the other's challenge, having heard all about what had happened later from the bartender. But he knew that most of his anger had been built on growing fear and uncertainty. Fear caught by the knowledge that this man, Denver, represented a greater challenge and menace to him than anyone he had known over the past years, that if he was not dealt with quickly, he might even get the nesters to form up against him, provide them with a leader and a cause.

Leaning back in his chair, legs thrust out straight in front of him to ease the dull ache in his body, an ache caused by the bruises he had received in the fist fight with Denver, he reflected that Cranshield had, perhaps, done just as he had ordered him to. Not to interfere at all in what was a private battle between himself and Denver. But damn it all, he thought fiercely, surely the other should have realised that when he had given that order he had been absolutely certain that he could whip Denver even with one hand tied behind his back. Once the other had seen that Denver was the victor, he should have challenged him there and then, shot him down, and rid him of this menace for good. Now Denver was still alive, and God alone knew what damage he might do if he stayed around in town long enough.

Reaching forward, he rang the small silver bell that stood on the table beside him.

A few moments later, one of the Negro servants appeared and stood patiently waiting just inside the room.

'Find Cranshield and tell him I want him here right away,' Marsden said harshly. 'You'll find him near the corral.'

Five minutes later, the foreman came into the room. He stood by the window with his hat in his hands. There was a sullen look on Cranshield's face as he waited for the other to speak. Marsden always tended to overlook the other's habits, knowing that Cranshield always looked upon himself as an equal and not as servant and master. But there was no doubt that Cranshield was a loyal segundo, that he had always stood by him since the beginning when he had set up this place and built it up into what it was now.

'You ever heard of this *hombre* who calls himself Denver?'

Cranshield pressed his lips together tightly, then shook his head in negation. 'Might not be his real name,' he said at length.

'Possibly. I get the impression he's another of these wild boys from the south, ridin' through and hell-bent for trouble. Normally I'd leave it up to Parker to run him out of town or see to it that he makes no more trouble. But I figure he's maybe too tough a nut for Parker to crack.'

'You want me to take care of him?' There was a deceptive mildness to the other's voice.

Marsden fixed the foreman with a sharp-bright glance. 'What's the general opinion on Denver?'

The other hesitated, took time over the reply. After a long consideration, he said: 'It's allowed that he could be dangerous. He carries his guns as if he knows how to use 'em. General opinion is that he's just another hell-raiser up from Texas, tryin' to make his mark here before movin' on again.'

'That your verdict on him too?' Marsden's eyes were brighter than before.

'I ain't sure about him. Somethin' familiar, but I can't say what it is. There's talk that he was in with the nesters out at Long Valley when he rode in this way. Seemed to be on mighty friendly terms with 'em.'

'That just after you tried to smoke the homesteaders out?'

Cranshield gave a quick nod. 'That's right. You reckon

he's willin' to throw in his lot with those critters?'

'If he is, then he's more of a menace to me than I figured. He'll be all set to buck us from sun-up to sundown. Maybe he wants to show these folk what an all-fired hero he is. Trouble is, if he's as good as he looks then he could make things real tough for us. I want him out of the way before that happens.'

Cranshield nodded confidently. 'I'll attend to that,' he said briskly. 'I've never let you down before whenever gunmen like this have tried to set themselves up against us, have I?'

'No, that's true, and I'm only sorry I told you not to horn in last night. Guess it was because I wanted to get revenge on him in my own way.'

'He still in town?' inquired the foreman. He hooked his thumbs inside his gunbelt, stood with his legs braced slightly apart.

'Was the last I heard of him. Take your mount and ride out there right away. No tellin' what he might be gettin' up to if he starts out. As for these nesters. . . Only one way to handle them and I intend to do it, but I have to be sure that Denver is out of the way first. I've got the say in Culver Creek and there ain't nobody goin' to say otherwise.'

Cranshield had heard most of this before, not once but several times. He gave a quick nod of agreement. 'We've done pretty well so far in Culver Creek, it would be a pity for somebody like this to horn in and spoil it all.' His grin was savage and vicious. His fingers rubbed the butts of the guns in their holsters.

'Just fix it so that he's no longer a danger to us,' said Marsden uncompromisingly.

'I'll do just that.' Turning on his heel, Cranshield left, closing the door quietly behind him. Marsden sat back in his chair and lit a thin, black cheroot, blowing the smoke through his nostrils. He listened to the sound of the other's booted heels fade into the distance, then cease

69

altogether as the foreman stepped down from the porch into the dust of the courtyard. There was a sense of satisfaction deep within him. Already, he had dismissed Denver from his mind, confident that there would no longer be a problem there.

Jeff sat on the low wooden bench around the trunk of the tall cottonwood on the edge of town. It was the heat of the early afternoon and here was the only place where there was a little coolness, where the faint breeze that drifted along the main street did not seem as if it had been dragged over some vast oven before it reached him.

The town had been quiet for most of the day after the furore of the previous evening. He had half expected Marsden to make his play that morning, but the hours had passed and nothing had happened. Now he was beginning to wonder whether or not the other might have decided to hold his hand until he saw a little more of what Jeff might have in mind riding into Culver Creek. It didn't fit in with the other's character as Jeff had seen it in the saloon. The fact that Marsden had deliberately picked that fight with him without much reason indicated that his temper was quick and sudden, that he was a man given to uncontrollable rages at times.

Now, with the warmth of the sun on his back and shoulders and the faint touch of the breeze on his face, he tried to put his thoughts into some sort of order, to think things out and decide what he was going to do. He no longer doubted that the three men he was after had signed on the Triple Bar payroll and this being the case, it was not going to be easy to prise them loose. They had discovered some kind of haven for themselves and they would stick with it until a chance came for them to attack him, relying on the backing of the other men in the outfit. With Marsden gunning for him, it seemed a safe bet they could rely on this.

To try to ride out and force the issue would be madness. He would have to fight cunning with cunning, and stealth with stealth. He turned his head and looked up at the sound of someone walking towards him, boots scuffing in the ankle-deep dust. Eyes narrowed down against the vicious sun glare, he saw that it was one of the boys from the store near the middle of town.

The lad came right up to him, gave him a close stare, then asked: 'You Jeff Denver?'

'That's right, son.' Jeff gave a quick nod. 'What's on your mind?'

'Ed Cranshield is in town. He's askin' around for you. Says that he'll be waitin' in the saloon unless you're too yeller to come.'

Jeff tightened his lips. He had no fight with Cranshield, but he could guess at the reason behind this challenge. Marsden had decided to make his play and he had sent his fast gun to do the dirty work for him. Getting to his feet, he dug into the pocket of his shirt, pressed the silver dollar into the boy's outstretched palm. 'Thanks,' he said quietly. 'Tell him I'll be along right away.'

The other gazed in awe at the money shining in his hand. Then he gave Jeff a quick, bird-like glance, his eyes bright. 'He's a real killer, mister. I've seen him gun down two men in the street.'

Clapping the boy on the shoulder, Jeff gave a grin. 'I've no doubt you have,' he said easily. 'But there always seems to come a time when a man runs up against a gun that's faster than his. Maybe that's what's goin' to happen to Cranshield today.'

'I sure hope so,' nodded the other. He hesitated for a second, then closed his fingers into a tight fist around the dollar and ran off, feet kicking up tiny spurts of yellow-white dust. Jeff remained quite still, watching as the other raced back along the quiet, empty street, paused for a moment then turned and go inside the saloon.

71

Slowly, he made his way back into town, feeling the burning heat on his face now that the buildings on either side shielded him from the cooling breeze. Inwardly, he felt little. There was a strange emptiness in his mind, and apart from that, he experienced nothing more. The stillness in the town was almost a physical thing now, pressing in on him from both sides. He had the feeling that there were eyes watching his every move as he strode along the main street, but whenever he turned his head a little to stare up at the windows which looked down on the road, he saw no movement there.

As he was passing the sheriff's office, the door swung open, causing him to whirl swiftly, instinctively. Parker came out, paused for a moment staring across at him without any expression on his face. Then he walked over and said softly: 'I heard about Cranshield, Denver. He's a cold-blooded killer. I warned you though of the trouble you were gettin' into if you persisted in stayin' here against my advice. If you'd just ridden out yesterday when I gave you the chance, this would never have happened.'

'Just you stay out of this little matter, Sheriff,' Jeff said harshly. 'It happens to be somethin' just between Cranshield and me.' He tightened his lips for a moment. 'I just want you to know that he's called me out. You try to arrest me on any charge just because Marsden says so and I'll kill you.'

He saw the other's features blanch at that and then colour with a sudden rush of anger. Speaking through his teeth, Parker said: 'I was just givin' you some friendly advice, Denver. Seems to me that you don't need it. Just that I didn't want to see some other stranger killed like this. But you seem to be determined about it, so go to hell and be damned with you.' He turned brusquely on his heel and strode back towards his office, going inside and slamming the door behind him.

Shrugging his shoulders, Jeff continued on towards the

saloon, mounted the boardwalk, pushed open the doors with the flat of his hand and went inside. It was too early for real business, but in spite of this the place seemed to be more crowded than usual. Ed Cranshield was standing at the bar drinking. He paused for a moment as he caught sight of Jeff's reflection in the bar, then tossed down his drink as if nothing had happened, kept his back to the other.

Jeff walked slowly forward, aware of the eyes on his every move, went up to the bar and motioned to the bartender. The other paused, gave Cranshield a quick look, then came over to where Jeff stood.

'Whisky,' Jeff said tautly.

The other put the bottle and a glass on the counter in front of him and then moved away almost as though Jeff was the victim of some contagious disease. Pouring himself a drink, Jeff drank it in a single gulp, glanced at Cranshield out of the edge of his vision. The foreman had evidently been drinking already. His face was flushed, his eyes bright. But his hand was steady as he set down his empty glass.

'I hear you've been lookin' for me, Cranshield,' Jeff said as the silence stretched out almost to breaking point. 'You got somethin' on your mind?'

Cranshield did not answer at once, but stood propped against the bar, whirling his glass in his hands. Then he turned his head in a leisurely fashion to stare at Jeff. 'You've been causin' a heap of trouble in town since you rode in, Denver,' he said through thinned lips. 'Mister Marsden has asked me to do somethin' about it.'

Jeff grinned. 'I've got nothin' against you personally, Cranshield,' he said, his tone high and challenging. 'And I don't particularly want to kill you. I came into town for somethin' quite different. But if you're so goddamned anxious to die, I guess I shall have to accommodate you.'

There was an audible gasp from the onlookers. This was

something very few of them had expected to hear. This stranger who had ridden into town only a day or so earlier had already beaten Marsden, reputed to be one of the strongest and roughest fighters in the territory and now he was here, challenging the terrible gunfighter of the Triple Bar ranch. Many of them remembered the inevitable outcome of previous gunfights they had seen when Cranshield had gone out hunting down other gunslingers, men who figured they were faster than he was with a gun. Now, it seemed it was all happening again.

The bartender moved away from the counter, stood with his back and shoulders pressed tightly against the mirror on the wall, his eyes wide. There was a scattergun kept just under the bar for trouble such as this, but the thought of reaching for it and using it had not once entered his head on this occasion.

Across the room, the onlookers too were spreading out, so as not to be caught in the line of fire, once bullets started to fly. Very slowly Cranshield moved away from the bar, stood near one of the tables, his hands swinging loosely by his side, legs bent a little, shoulders drooping to give him less distance to move his hands when he went for his guns.

Cranshield smiled, stood relaxed, his empty, snake-like gaze fixed on Jeff's face. He began rubbing his fingers together slowly just in front of his gunbelt, eyes narrowed down somewhat taking on that crazy killer look that Jeff recognised.

'You're bein' paid money to kill me, Cranshield,' Jeff said, his voice very soft. 'Reckon you'd better try to earn it.'

Cranshield appeared to hesitate, keeping his eyes on Jeff, his lips twitching slightly. He ran the tip of his tongue around them as if they had suddenly gone quite dry. The truth of the matter was that he had never stacked up against a man of Jeff's apparent calibre before in the

whole of his career. He had known quite a lot about all of
the men he had faced in the past, had known their weak-
nesses and made due and proper allowance for them,
giving himself all the edge he needed thereby. Now, he felt
the first faint twinges of doubt,. Had he underestimated
this man who faced him so fearlessly? Was he one of those
fast killers like Billy the Kid, men who could draw and fire
three slugs into a man's chest before the other could draw
his guns clear of leather? His killer's courage was beginning to evaporate just a little.

Jeff's grin widened a little. He moved a couple of paces
towards the other so that it was now impossible for either
of them to miss and everything was resolved into a matter
of sheer speed of draw. 'You gettin' yeller?' Jeff asked
thinly.

Cranshield stood taut and curiously rigid. The crazy
look was still on his face and at the back of his eyes, but
some of the boldness had gone from him. He flicked a
quick glance in the direction of the group of men standing near the batwing doors, then looked equally swiftly
back at Jeff.

He said slowly: 'You seem to believe that you're a fast
man with a gun, Denver. Let's see just how fast you are.'
Even before he had finished speaking, evidently deciding
to take as much edge as possible, his hands flashed down
for the guns in their holsters. He got his fingers around
the polished walnut butts, was in the act of jerking them
free when Jeff's right hand moved. Striking down so
swiftly that it was impossible for any of the men in the
saloon to see it, he drew and fired in a single, smooth
movement. Cranshield suddenly stiffened and jerked as
the three slugs burned their way into his chest. He
teetered as the first one hit him, dropped his gun and
threw up his arms as though trying to claw at something
above his head as the other two hammered home, then
slumped on to his knees, blood pulsing from his lips as

he crashed forward on to the floor at Jeff's feet.

There was a stunned, muffling silence in the saloon as the echoes of the three gunshots faded away. Through the blue haze of gunsmoke, the onlookers saw Jeff pouch his guns, then turn back to the bar, ignoring the inert body on the ground at his back. Picking up the bottle, he poured a second drink and sipped it slowly.

Reluctantly almost, the bartender edged forward, staring with a look of horrified bewilderment at Cranshield's dead body. Somebody said from the back of the room. 'Guess someone had better fetch the coroner. Ain't nothin' that the doctor can do for him. He's deader'n I've ever seen 'em.'

Less than three minutes later, the batwing doors crashed open and Parker strode into the saloon. He stared about him for a moment and then paced forward slowly, stood looking down at Cranshield's body for a long moment, then lifted his head to stare at Jeff.

'All right, what happened?' he snapped.

Jeff laughed at the sheriff's obvious discomfiture. He stared down the other. 'You know damned well what happened, Parker,' he said through tightly-clenches teeth. 'You know that he called me out. He drew first. I only fired in self-defence.'

'That ain't the way I see it,' Parker said. He reached down towards the gun at his waist, then froze. Quite suddenly, without seeing Jeff's hand move at all, he found himself staring down the ominous black hole in the barrel of the other's Colt. There was an ominous click as the hammer was drawn back.

'Seems to me you didn't hear right,' Jeff told the lawman. 'You'll find Cranshield's gun on the floor there.'

Block Parker lowered his gaze, his face stiff, white. Then he stared sullenly at Jeff before glancing at the bartender. 'What about it, Joe?'

The other swallowed, then said hastily, 'It's just like he

says, Sheriff. Cranshield drew first. This *hombre* beat him to the draw. I ain't never seen anythin' like it.'

Jeff laughed at the sheriff's obvious discomfiture. He said harshly: 'I can understand your position, Parker. Soon as word of this gets back to Marsden he's goin' to want to know why you didn't arrest me on a charge of murder. I don't envy you your job in town. Trouble is that Marsden has got you all so scared that you jump at every shadow. You ain't the law in Culver Creek, Parker. You never have been. Marsden gives the orders and you jump to make sure they're carried out. How much longer are you goin' to let him run your lives and keep you under his thumb?'

For a moment there was a strange expression on Parker's face. He bit his lower lip, then said harshly, 'You don't know anythin' of what goes on in this part of the territory, Denver. You just ride into town and think you know everythin'. You ever seen a trail town that's been braced by cattlemen?' He shook his head slowly, bitterly. 'I guess not. Well I've seen it too many times not to know what happens. They burn it to the ground, shoot up everybody in sight. There are women and children in this town who'd have been dead long ago if I'd tried to fight Marsden and his gunfighters.'

Jeff said: 'So you fell in with him, did all of his dirty work for him as far as the town was concerned.'

'That's right,' snapped the other hoarsely. 'And I'd do the same again if I had to. I wasn't proud of it. No man is proud to act the way I had to act, to see lawlessness and murder carried out in front of his nose and know that if he tries to stop it, he'll be killed himself and the town burned. What good would my death do? Marsden would only find some other man willin' to take my place and do as he says. At least this way, I've been able to help a little.'

Jeff eyed the other closely. There was the ring of truth in what the other said. Maybe Parker had done as much as he could to steer lawlessness away from the town, to try to confine it to the territory outside where it would do the least damage as far as the townsfolk themselves were concerned.

He paused for just a second and then thrust the gun almost carelessly back into its holster. Parker wiped the sweat from his eyes and forehead, then looked back at Cranshield's body.

'It's fortunate for you there ain't any of the Triple Bar rannies in town right now. Guess that Marsden must've figured there'd be no trouble for Cranshield to handle you. But he won't make the same mistake the next time.'

'I'll be ready for him,' said Jeff confidently. 'Not that this town means anythin' to me. I rode here for one thing only. To get three men who betrayed me and my troop durin' the war. Once I've done that I'll be quite willin' to ride on out again and forget this place for good.'

'Which three men?' asked the sheriff warily. 'There were three *hombres* who rode in a couple of days or so before you arrived. They joined Marsden's outfit. Far as I know they're still ridin' with him.'

'They're the men I'm after,' Jeff muttered grimly.

'Then you won't find it easy to prise 'em loose from that bunch. One thing I'll say for Marsden and Cranshield. They took this bunch of killers and men on the run and they've bound themselves together into a tight-knit outfit who owe their loyalty only to Marsden, the man who gave them the sanctuary they were lookin' for.'

'There'll be a way to get at 'em.'

Parker shrugged his shoulders wearily. 'If there is, I don't see it myself, he answered. 'What do you figure on doin' now?' He seemed to have completely forgotten his original intention of arresting Jeff. There was the possibility that he considered Jeff more than able to take care of himself against anything that Marsden could send against him. Certainly if the word of the bartender was anything to go on, this man was the fastest man with a gun that he had ever heard of. Anyone who could put three slugs into a man like Ed Cranshield before the other had a chance to level his gun, was worth an earnest consideration.

'You got anythin' against the homesteaders?'

For a second, there was surprise on the lawman's face. Clearly he had not expected this sudden change of topic. He shrugged. 'They haven't caused me any trouble, or done anything in town,' he admitted finally. 'But that don't mean to say I like 'em.'

'Maybe not. But sooner or later you've got to live with them because they've got these plots of land legally from the Government and you won't be able to fight them off for ever. The time is comin' when they'll become a big part of this community and men like Marsden and the other ranchers will be unable to stop them.'

'Then you're throwin' in your hand with the nesters?'

'That's right. A man has got to fight for what he thinks is right. There's no doubt in my mind that Marsden is intent on forcin' these people off their rightful land, ready to grab off all the land and water for himself. And if the other ranchers who're aidin' him reckon that when the nesters are finished, they'll share the lot, then they're mistaken. Marsden sees no one here but himself. He'll get the edge on them and see to it that they don't have a chance.'

'How'd you light on these nesters in the first place?' asked Parker, suspicious.

'I saw some of Marsden's gunhawks bein' chased off from the valley while I was ridin' this way. Seems they ran into more than they'd bargained for.'

'It won't be that way the next time,' Parker told him. 'Marsden has never made the same mistake twice.'

'He did as far as I was concerned,' said Jeff grimly. 'When he hears that his top gun is no longer alive, that he's been deprived of that piece of comfort, he's goin' to have to take fast action, and when a man's bein' pushed like that, he's always inclined to act rashly and make mistakes. Things are movin' in on Marsden from all sides now. It started when he found he couldn't drive off the Fenners and their neighbours. It's been buildin' up on him over the past couple of days. Pretty soon, he's goin' to be a panicky man and he'll make the move that's goin' to be the end of him.'

As he spoke, he made his way past the sheriff, towards the door. 'If you're lookin' for me, Parker, I'll be in the hotel.'

For a long moment, the sheriff stared at him in surprise, as though he had not heard the other aright. 'You stayin' in town, even after that?' he asked incredulously.

'That's right. Don't see any reason to ride out just yet. Tomorrow I'll maybe pay a call on the Fenners again. I promised I'd ride back and let them know how things were goin'.' He thrust open the doors and stepped outside, leaving the other staring after him.

It was later that evening, sitting in his room at the hotel, that the first faint glimmering of a plan came to Jeff. The idea itself stemmed from what he recalled of the layout of the narrow valley in which the Fenners and their neighbours had built their homesteads and tilled their land. As he remembered it, the valley was bordered by the high hills, densely populated by the trees and thickly-tangled vegetation and with only the one narrow entrance with tall boulder-strewn rocky slopes on either side of it. If a bunch of men could be enticed into the valley and the defenders were strategically placed, they could close the gap behind them and destroy most of them with very little danger to themselves.

The difficulty was going to be to entice Marsden and his men into the valley in such a way that the trap could be sprung. After the beating his men had taken the last time they had attempted to shoot it out with the homesteaders, the Triple Bar riders would be wary, determined not to run into the same kind of trouble again.

On the other hand, if he could talk Fenner and the Shedden family into riding with him to carry out a night raid on Marsden's cattle, they might get the other sufficiently steamed up to throw all caution to the wind. It would certainly be the best form of defence, to attack the powerful Triple Bar ranch like that.

The more he turned the idea over in his mind, the more he figured that there was a real chance of it succeeding. It had the ring of the unexpected about it which always seemed to be a prerequisite to success. In spite of the fact that Cranshield was dead, Marsden would be confident that he still held the upper hand, that he had all of the high cards in his hands, and the homesteaders would be on the defensive. To hit him at night, drive off some of his cattle, would be a shock to him which would, or so Jeff figured, force him to act precipitously.

Once he had the other on the run like that, they would be committed to hammering him without respite, keeping him on the defensive, so that he would be unable to bring his superior force of gunmen against them. There was then the very definite chance that they might whittle down the Triple Bar outfit down to a par with their own force: Clint Shedden and his five sons would be a welcome addition to the small force they could raise against Marsden, provided the other agreed to fall in with the plan.

CHAPTER 5

THE MARK OF VIOLENCE

Jeff rose early the next morning, before it was light, left the hotel and went along to the livery stables. He had to shake the groom awake and the other got his mount for him with plenty of grumbling under his breath. But ten minutes later it was ready and saddled and he swung up with a lithe movement. He came to the low ridge which overlooked the entrance to the valley less than a mile away just as the sun was lifting from behind the tall, craggy rocks. Here, he paused briefly, taking in everything in a sweeping glance. His memory of the place had not been at fault. If anything, the terrain suited his plan even better than he had dared hope. The shallow basin which fronted the entrance to the valley was covered in coarse grass and here and there were a few stunted trees which could afford cover to a man keeping a sharp look out for any approaching riders. Further back, the ground sloped downward into the valley and the entrance itself was so narrow that he doubted if three men would be able to ride abreast through it.

On either side of the narrow pass, the rocky walls lifted

sheer above the ground. They were even higher and more formidable than he had remembered, eminently suited to a small bunch of men, sited among the rocks, able to shoot down on the Triple Bar crew if they tried to ride out through the pass.

Gigging his mount forward, he rode slowly along the winding trail, reached a point that was bare of any vegetation, then swung off the trail, out into the valley which opened out before him in the pearly light which was rapidly becoming red as the sun rose. There was still a refreshing coolness in the air and he drew in deep breaths, letting it go down and fill his lungs.

He arrived at the two homesteads an hour before high noon with the heat beginning to flood down into the valley, caught and trapped by the high walls of rock and vegetation. With a faint sense of surprise, he noticed that there was a new house being built some quarter of a mile from the other two and from that distance he was able to make out the two men who had hammered thick posts into the ground and were now busily stringing wire between them, fencing off their plot of ground. The covered wagon which had brought them there was settled down in the tall grass, with a couple of horses grazing peaceably nearby and a woman with a shawl around her shoulders near the narrow stream, scrubbing clothes on a long wooden board.

Hal Fenner came out to meet him as he slid from his horse and let it wander towards the nearby grass. He gave Jeff a warm smile of greeting.

'You're back sooner than we expected,' he called. 'Any trouble in Culver Creek?'

Jeff gave a brief nod, brought out the makings of a smoke and stood with his back against one of the wooden uprights. Briefly, he told the other of all that had happened during the past few days, of his talk with the sheriff and the shoot-out with Ed Cranshield. When he had finished Fenner said:

'You say that Cranshield is dead? That you outdrew him?'

Jeff lit his cigarette and drew deeply on it. 'He's dead all right. But this may force Marsden into makin' a move against you and the others. I see that more folk have arrived yonder.' He gestured towards the group a short distance away.

'Came the day before yesterday,' Fenner muttered. 'Haven't met 'em yet, but no doubt they'll come over if they want to borrow somethin'. At the moment they're pretty busy settin' everythin' up.' His face grew more serious. 'But you were sayin' that maybe Marsden is plannin' somethin' against us. What you got on your mind?'

'I'm not sure what he'll try to do. He'll most likely ride into Culver Creek to try to find me and when he discovers I'm no longer there, he'll come out this way, lookin' for me.'

Fenner pursed his lips. 'You can count on us to back you if he does come this way.'

'There's more in it than that,' Jeff told him. 'I figure we'd better talk this thing over. It could be that we have a chance to smash Marsden once and for all. But I'd need not only your help, but Shedden's and anyone else who can handle a gun and ain't scared to do so.'

Fenner drew his thick, black brows together. 'Let's go inside,' he said, motioning towards the door. 'You'll be hungry after your ride and Susan can get you somethin' to eat. Then you can tell me what you've got on your mind.'

Pushing his empty plate away, Jeff leaned back in his chair, stared across the table at Susan Fenner. 'That was one of the best meals I've ever tasted, Susan,' he said quietly. 'I guess I was even more hungry than I'd figured.'

'We're a little short of most of the luxuries of life at the moment,' she remarked. 'But sooner or later, we'll have them. Once these people have accepted us here as part of the community. Somehow, I can't see why they are so set against us. I can understand the cattlemen not liking us here. They've regarded this open range as theirs for so long that they seem to forget that they have no legal right to it. But the townsfolk ought to know that we're peaceable people, and that we can do a great deal of trade with them.'

'I dare say that you'd find they were friendly enough in the ordinary way. Trouble is that it's Marsden and the other ranchers who hold the whip hand in this territory. They bring in gunhawks from all over the State. Anyone who is fast with a gun and is on the run from the law signs on their payroll and they have a private army of killers who'll do just as they're ordered. Once the townsfolk step out of line, Marsden will simply order his men to ride in and fire the town. That's what they're afraid of. Even Sheriff Parker has realised that and does as he's told. If he didn't, he knows what the consequences will be.'

'Jeff is right, Susan,' said her father gruffly. 'This is frontier territory and the laws we knew back east just don't apply here. It's the law of violence and the six-gun which carries all the weight in these parts and we have to recognise that fact.'

'But surely the Government—' began the girl.

Jeff shook his head emphatically. 'The Government is in Washington, many hundreds of miles away from here,' he explained. 'They don't have the men, or the inclination, to bring proper law and order here. Maybe in ten years things will be different. Then the frontier will have been pushed even further west and we'll have federal officers and straight-shootin' sheriffs who aren't afraid to stand up to these killers.'

'But in the meantime we either have to knuckle under to Marsden and men like him or be killed. Is that it?' There was a defiant tilt to the girl's chin and her eyes flashed brightly as she regarded him steadily.

Jeff forced a grim smile. 'There is one alternative open to us,' he said softly, very quiet. 'That's why I came out here, to talk it over with your father. We can fight cunning with cunning and fix things so that we get on even terms with Marsden and the others.'

He saw her slender brows come together in perplexity. 'I'm not sure that I understand you,' she said.

'Has it ever occurred to you that this valley would make a natural trap for any bunch of riders who rode in after you? If you had men sited on the hills overlooking the entrance and others around the valley it would be possible to empty most of their saddles and force them to run a gauntlet of fire before they could have any chance of escape.'

Fenner saw the force of the argument at once. He nodded slowly. 'You're right. The idea has got a chance. But if the deal doesn't go our way, we could find ourselves in a lot of trouble. Besides, how do you intend to get that gun slinging crew into the valley in the first place.'

'I've got me an idea about that too,' Jeff told him. 'I figure it's about time that somebody struck back at Marsden.'

'How?'

'If Shedden will throw in his lot with us, I reckon we'd make a good enough band to rustle some of Marsden's beef and drive 'em into the valley. If that doesn't bring the outfit after us, I guess nothin' will.'

'You suggestin' that we should ride against Marsden?' asked Fenner incredulously.

'That's right. If Shedden and his boys will ride with us, that makes eight. We could hit them and drive off their cattle after dark before they know that anythin' is up.'

'Don't you think it might be better to leave some behind, just in case they follow you close?' put in the girl. 'If they do, you may not have much time to position men among the rocks.'

'That's certainly a point worth considerin',' nodded Jeff. 'It means splittin' our forces, but that can't be helped.' He got to his feet. 'Reckon we'd better have a talk with Shedden and his boys. All of this is goin' to depend on him helpin' us.'

'Ain't no love lost between him and Marsden as you well know,' Fenner said, leading the way to the door.

Jeff gave a tight, grim nod. He had almost forgotten that it had been mainly the actions of Shedden and his sons which had scared off Marsden's outfit when they attacked the homesteaders before.

Shedden, burly and black-bearded, readily agreed to throw in with them apparently only too anxious to have this chance of fighting back at Marsden after all the other had done and threatened to do. It was agreed that Shedden and three of his boys would stay behind, ready among the rocks which guarded the entrance of the valley, while Jeff, Fenner and the others rode out after dark to drive off part of Marsden's herd.

Sundown; and the four riders forded the river and climbed up on to the trail once more. There were long, black shadows lying over the terrain through which they rode and Jeff flicked his gaze from one side of the trail to the other, alert and watchful. They were still some distance from the perimeter wire of the Triple Bar spread, two or three miles he judged and they appeared to have figured things just right. By the time they came within sight of the nearest of Marsden's line camps, it would be almost completely dark.

The trail slid across a sharply-angled ravine, then came out to the break-off point in this string of hills and Jeff, sitting forward in the saddle, saw the slope roll far down until it met a wide, natural basin about a mile across, on the far side of which stood a dark rim. There, he reflected, was the timber line, the dividing line between these rugged hills and the Triple Bar ranch. Through the last hazy rim of daylight, he glimpsed the higher mountains far off on the horizon, jagged peaks that lifted sheer to the western skies. The sun had vanished in flame and violence and now there was the denser blackness of night sweeping in swiftly from the east, with the first of the sky sentinels just showing.

Crossing the shallow depression, they put their mounts to the steep climb on the far side, heading for the timberline. Around the four horsemen, the desert and hills stood silent and dark. Out of the stillness, broken only by the muffled hoofbeats of their horses, came the sudden-soft voice of Hal Fenner.

'Can't be much further. Just over the rim of the hills yonder.'

Jeff sat straighter in the saddle, felt his nervous alertness increase as they continued to move up with the slope of the hills. Here and there, they passed shallow alkali sinks which showed whitely in the gloom and there were narrow cattle trails which led down to the mud. The rattle of their horses' hoofs became more thinly-echoing as the ground underfoot became stony, laced here and there with long wide patches of smooth shale.

A yellow-white moon rose twenty minutes later, flooded the forest of ash and pine through which they were riding with light. Jet Shedden, leading them in single file, suddenly reined up and lifted his right hand. Slowly, Jeff came alongside him, peered forward into the gloom. He sat silent for a long moment, attuning his ears to the faint night sounds all about them, the furtive rustle of a nocturnal creature in the thickly tangled undergrowth which grew beneath the trees.

In the shadows, the wide-brimmed hat which the other wore, completely shielded his face. He said in a harsh tone: 'The Triple Bar beeves are just over the rise yonder.'

'I wonder how many riders are runnin' nursemaid to 'em,' Jeff grunted.

'Five or six, I'd say,' muttered Fenner as he lifted himself a little in the saddle. 'That's the usual number Marsden has in his line camps. Can't see any reason why he'd double the guard. He can't be expectin' us.'

Jeff grinned faintly. 'That's for sure,' he acknowledged. 'This is the last thing he'd expect us to do. That's why I figure we've got a good chance of pullin' it off.' Gently, he edged his mount forward, the horse's hoofs making no sound at all in the soft earth which lay beneath the trees. Atop the low ridge, he halted, searched the gloom of the long meadow which opened out in front of him until he sighted the dark, irregular shadow of the herd. He guessed there to be somewhat less than a thousand head of cattle there, bedded down for the night in a wide, shallow depression some half a mile away. Off to his right, the yellow-orange gleam of a camp fire gave away the presence of the line crew. By the faintly flickering light of the flames he was able to make out the shapes of three horses standing patiently, ground-reined, close by. He could not see the owners of those horses, but if Fenner was right that left three men riding herd.

'There they are,' said Fenner softly, coming forward. He pointed a hand. 'And there are the guards.'

Narrowing his eyes, Jeff was just able to make out the distant shapes of the three riders, circling the herd on the side most distant from them. For a moment, the uneasiness stirred again deep within him. There were quite a lot of things which could go wrong with this plan of his in spite of its relative simplicity. That camp fire was a little too close to the herd for his liking. Once trouble started, they would be able to mount up and ride out to help their companions pretty quickly. He had hoped for a little more time before there was any real pursuit.

It required a moment for him to force his mind back

into its normal rut, but Jeff did it with his sense of urgency deepening. So far, there was no indication that they had been seen. He reckoned that none of the men would be more than usually watchful. They would never expect anyone to try to rustle the Triple Bar herd.

'How'd you figure we ought to hit that herd, Jeff?' Fenner's moonlit face was turned sideways as he glanced speculatively over the long meadow.

'Oughtn't to be too difficult to spook part of it,' Jeff murmured. 'I reckon our best bet would be to try to drive the main part towards that line camp, splitting off a decent bunch and herdin' them this way.'

Fenner nodded and Jeff saw that the other two men were doing the same. He knew that this was probably the first time any of them had done anything like this. Mostly, the nesters were only too keen to stay on the right side of the law, unless something happened which made them fight any way they were able. But he did not doubt that once they were committed, they would back him to he hilt.

Tightening his grip momentarily on the reins, he said with a faint, savage hiss. 'Right, let's go get 'em. Hal, you take Jet and drive the herd over in the direction of the camp, Hank and I will move around to the other side, split off fifty or a hundred and herd them over here. If any of the hands try to interfere, then just remember that these men are hired killers with a price on their heads and that they'll be shootin' to kill.'

'You don't need to tell us that, ' grunted Jet Shedden. 'These are likely the same men who rode out a few days ago and tried to burn us to the ground. We ain't forgotten any of that.'

'Good.' Jeff gave a brief nod. Touching spurs to the horse's flanks, he urged it forward, saw out of the corner of his eye, Fenner and Jet Shedden ride over to his left, just visible in the dimness.

It took a little longer than Jeff had reckoned to split up

the bunch. The other two men had swung around swiftly, hazing in at the milling cattle, yelling and shooting off their guns as they rode forward, stampeding the drowsy beasts towards the camp fire that gleamed brightly in the distance. For several moments, the steers bawled and lunged, milling around without settling down to head in any one direction. Then a lead steer moved, reluctantly, head lowered, needle-sharp horns just missing Fenner's leg as he swung his horse out of the way. The next minute, all hell would not have held them as countless tons of beef, sinew and muscle thundered towards the line camp.

Only vaguely was Jeff aware of the shrill cries of alarm that came from the camp as the men there realised their danger. Surprise must have been virtually complete for the three men there as they struggled up from their evening meal and ran for their mounts, striving desperately to unloosen their reins and swing up into the saddle, knowing they had only moments to move out and away from the thundering avalanche of solid fury which was descending on them out of the yellow moonlight.

But Jeff saw nothing of this. All of his attention was now centred on the small bunch which Hank Shedden had succeeded in splitting out from the main herd, driving them off to the right towards the distant rim of rock where the trees lifted dark against the skyline.

'Hold it!'

The shrill shout brought Jeff lifting, alert, in the saddle, and he swung his body sharply to where the three riders came spurring their mounts forward. Almost at once, the wicked blue-crimson flare of a gun spat out from the darkness. Pandemonium broke loose as the Triple Bar riders came thundering forward, firing as they came. Jeff fought his mount savagely as it began to rear, bucking and saw-fishing, realising the danger which came from riding a spooked horse with all of these cattle stampeding around, not to mention the riders closing in on them, fanning out swiftly as they tried to head them off.

Jerking his Colt from its holster, Jeff fired a couple of shots at the men, saw one of them sway drunkenly in the saddle. For a moment the man almost managed to stay upright. then his body tilted to one side and he went down, his fear-crazed horse dragging him for several yards where his boot was caught in one stirrup. Then his leg came loose and he toppled into the dust, lying still where he had fallen.

Drawing a quick bead on one of the other men, he yelled at Hank to keep the cattle moving, to leave him to take care of the riders. Out of the corner of his vision, he saw the other's burly shape sitting easily on his mount, driving the cattle away from the main herd which was, by now, thundering down on the camp. Firing a couple of quick shots, he saw the man weave but he did not go down. Gun-flare leapt at Jeff from the third rider as the other came swinging in. He swung his gun again, fired until the hammer clicked dully on an empty chamber, then wheeled his mount away.

Yelling, the rider ran his horse at full tilt. Jeff could see the other's face beneath the wide-brimmed hat, his grin a vicious gleam in the shadow of his features. Almost casually, the other man lifted his gun, aiming it at Jeff. He saw the spurt of fire from the barrel, jerked himself back in the saddle, almost unseating himself. The slug touched his sleeve, burned its way along the flesh of his right arm. Sucking in air through his clenched teeth, he fought down the gasp of pain. He guessed that the other still had some slugs left in his gun. There was only one way to save his life now and he moved swiftly and instinctively. To have tried to run would have meant committing suicide, getting a slug in the middle of his back.

Jerking on the reins, he whirled his horse straight for the others, matching it's stride for stride. The move took the gunhawk completely by surprise. His mouth open, he tried to lift his gun, to bring it into line, but the distance was short now and before he could line up the barrel and squeeze the trigger, Jeff had leaned sideways in the saddle, his own gun reversed, fingers gripping it tightly by the barrel.

Using it as a club, he brought the butt crashing down on the man's head, felt the sickening crunch as the heavy metal struck the other a savage, vicious blow. The man reeled without a single cry, lifted one hand instinctively, but he was already unconscious. Sliding from the saddle, he crashed to the ground beneath the flailing hoofs of his horse.

The riderless horse ran on into the darkness and Jeff pulled his mount round swiftly, heading towards the tree-lined ridge. The first steers were already moving over the top of the ledge, like a mass of dark water flowing down the rocky slope. Hank Shedden was a dim shadow, driving them forward. There was no sign of the man he had wounded and for a second a twinge of doubt ran through his mind. He felt certain that his shot had not killed the other, had probably not even badly wounded him.

Back at the line camp, there seemed to be all hell let loose. Red gun flashes spat in the darkness. The fire seemed to have been scattered in all directions and there was no sign of the men who had been eating there when the stampeding herd had crashed down on them, carrying all before it.

A sudden movement at the corner of his eye caught his attention. Swiftly thumbing fresh shells into the Colt, he watched the two riders heading towards them, jerked up the Colt, finger tight on the trigger, then relaxed as he saw it was Fenner and Jet Shedden.

'We won't have any trouble from the three back there,' yelled Fenner exultantly. 'They're too busy tryin' to get out of the way of the herd. Even when they catch up with it, it'll be a while before they decide to come after us.'

'Then once we get these critters out of the timber and through the rocks, we'll take our time,' Jeff said. 'I want to be sure that they do follow us. All of this will have been in vain if they don't come after us.'

'Sure,' nodded the other grimly. 'But they'll come. Word will get back to Marsden within the hour of what has happened, and he won't wait before sendin' his entire bunch after us.'

'That's what we want,' Jeff muttered. They reached the ledge, tipped their horses over the lip of rock and rode down into the cool darkness of the trees. The bawling, thunderous roar of the stampeded herd was fading into the distance behind them, while in front, the steers they had driven off were moving more docilely along the rocky trail.

It was a couple of hours later, a little after midnight, as they were driving the herd across the open stretch of desert fronting the valley, that the first intimation of pursuit reached them. Jeff straightened in the saddle, turning slowly. The gentle, slow, scrubbing sound came from the north-west; a large bunch of riders moving on a trail which slanted towards them for the sound grew greater even as he stood there.

'Get those cattle movin' a little faster,' he called. 'Sounds like Marsden and his men on our tail.'

The other men needed no urging. Within moments the huge beasts were moving at a lumbering run, not liking it, knowing that this was the time when they were normally bedded down on some green pasture and not dragging their feet through the dry dust of the desert. Bawling angrily, they snorted along the trail, heads swinging massively from side to side, kicking up a cloud of dust which Jeff knew would give away their position to the riders behind them as surely as if the gunhawks could see each individual beast.

The entrance to the valley was now less than half a mile ahead and he threw a speculative glance over his shoulder, striving to pick out the dust cloud thrown up by the approaching riders, to estimate how much time they had left once they hit the valley. The idea then was to send the herd scattering forward and then move up the rocky slopes to take their own places among the boulders, ready to add their fire to that of the men already in position.

Halfway to the valley, with still a quarter of a mile to go, he spotted the dust of their pursuers and at the same moment, saw the brief gunflashes as the Triple Bar riders commenced to fire at them. The distance was far too great for revolvers, possibly even for rifles and none of the fire came close to them as they urged on the cattle at an even greater pace. Racing his mount forward, Jeff rode alongside the huge, bawling beasts, spinning flame from his guns into their eyes, starting them to run again, forcing them along at an even quicker pace in spite of their protests. The other riders emptied their guns, knowing that now everything depended on getting the cattle through that narrow gap and into the valley before the Triple Bar riders caught up with them.

The four riders held rigidly to either side of the herd. It was almost a stampede, but not quite. The steers were still under control, were still headed in the right direction.

Fifteen minutes were gone – minutes which seemed to drag themselves out through an eternity. The lead steers were now moving through the narrow pass. The rest of the small herd followed them. As he rode, Jeff felt a sense of relief course through him, driving some of the weariness from his body. The first part of his plan had gone off without a hitch. But there was still a lot to do and a lot that could go wrong.

The last of the herd went through, their bawling echoes thrown back at them from the looming rocky walls. Then Jeff rode behind them, felt the high rock walls close in on him for a long moment, knew a strange sense of being hemmed in. Then he was through, the herd was sent scattering into the darkness, now needing no cajoling as they smelled the lush green grass which grew there and the water from the narrow river half a mile distant.

'Up into the rocks,' Jeff called harshly. 'Those *hombres* will be ridin' into the valley in minutes.'

Tugging savagely at the reins, he spurred his horse forward, off the trail and up to his left. Fenner was close behind him, kicking spurs at his horse's heaving flanks. The Shedden boys took the other side. In places, the pathway pitched so steeply that it seemed impossible for the horse to make it; but somehow, tired though it was, it succeeded in scrambling through the loose rocks, up on to the narrow ledge thirty feet above the valley floor. In the pitch blackness, it would have been suicidal to try to go any further on horseback. Dropping lightly from the saddle, he waited for Hal Fenner to come up to him, then they moved towards the end of the ledge, keeping their heads well down, pressing in tightly against the wall of rock on their left, knowing that in places the ledge was less than two feet in width and one false move could send them hurtling to the rocks below and certain death.

At the end of the ledge, the cliff was rock and earth with scant vegetation growing out of the thin topsoil, somehow struggling to survive in these unfriendly conditions. Night wind blew down from the higher ledges, cool in their faces.

Three minutes later, they rounded a bulging outcrop of rock and came upon the two men crouched there in the shadows, rifles laid ready in narrow V's in the rocks. The nearer of the two turned.

'You get on all right, Jeff?' asked Shedden gruffly. 'We've been lyin' here for the past hour or so, waitin' for you to show up. Reckon that was part of the herd that went through a little while ago.'

'That's right.' Sucking air down into his lungs, Jeff gave a tight nod. 'The Marsden bunch are only a little way behind us. Could be that they'll be a little wary about ridin' into the valley after what happened to 'em the last time. Depends on how sure they feel of themselves, I guess.'

'Here they come now,' muttered Slim Shedden. He pointed off to his right to the valley entrance.

Jeff pushed his sight through the clinging darkness. Here, the moonlight was cut off by the sheer rising wall of rock and a deep shadow lay over the floor of the valley. He could just make out the tightly-packed bunch of riders approaching across the desert. When they were less than two hundred yards from the valley entrance, the men stopped, reining up their mounts sharply.

'Looks to me as if they ain't too sure of whether to come on or not,' Shedden said thinly. He touched the stock of his rifle. 'Do we let 'em ride on in before we open up?'

'That's the plan.' Jeff wiped the sweat off his forehead with the back of his sleeve. 'Whatever happens, don't open up until they're well inside. We don't want to give any of 'em the chance of ridin' back out again. Let 'em ride in as if nothin' is wrong and then we'll snap the trap shut behind 'em.'

Marsden's party was now moving forward at a slower pace than before and as they drew nearer to the narrow opening in the rocks, they strung themselves out in single file, evidently taking no chances, moving with utmost caution. He took his rifle and crouched down, steadying the gun on the rocks in front of him, squinting along the sights. He judged that by the time those men were well inside the valley, they would be within killing distance of revolvers as well as the high-powered rifles. With his men positioned on both sides of the trail, it would be possible to send down a massed, lethal hail of fire on those riders, throwing them into confusion and emptying most of their saddles with the first volley.

The party drifted on until they came to the entrance where they paused again. The horses now stood nose to tail, crowded together, and to Jeff it seemed that some man in the centre of the column, more nervous than the others was beginning to complain about the delay. Evidently it had occurred to him that once they were through and into the wide valley they would have far more room in which to manoeuvre than they had just at that point, and he was clearly afraid that if there was an ambush, it would be just at the entrance where they were all crowded into one thick bunch, laying themselves open to intense fire.

'What in tarnation are they waitin' for now?' hissed Shedden thinly. He shifted himself into a more comfortable position, lying full length behind his rifle, staring along the sights, his finger very close to the trigger guard but not actually inside it.

'They'll move, just as soon as they're sure it isn't a trap,' Jeff said softly. 'Hold you fire. If anyone opens up now, we'll have lost more than half of 'em and I want to kill as many as I can. This is the only way to even things up a little, maybe swing the advantage on to our side.'

'They're movin' now,' whispered Slim.

Down below, the column had formed up once again and were edging their way through the narrow pass into the valley. Jeff watched them closely, noticing the way in which they moved more quickly once they were through and into the open. By now they seemed to have become convinced that there was no trap, that the men who had rustled and driven off the cattle had moved them further into the valley. He could almost imagine their confidence returning with a rush as they found themselves in the valley and still alive, still no lead thrown at them. The distant lowing of the herd came to them a few moments later, borne on the breeze that drifted along the valley. One of the men down below lifted an arm to point.

The last man in the column worked his way through the pass, joined up with the rest, and the party, bunched again, began to move forward. Jeff placed his finger on the trigger of the Winchester, waited for a moment, feeling only the beat of the blood in his temples. He waited and took up the trigger's slack, holding his breath. An instant later, he found the shoulders of one of the men in the notch of his sights, and let go. The thunderous sound of the rifle shot bucketed back and forth from the rocks on either side of the trail. Down below, the rider lurched in his saddle and then toppled to one side, rolling out of sight behind his mount.

Other rifles cracked from among the rocks on either side of the valley mouth in an irregular volley, spitting lead at the men down below. Two men tried to ride their mounts back for the narrow pass, were shot from their saddles before they could reach it and only the two rider-less horses raced through, vanishing into the moonlight that flooded the desert.

Shouts of rage and fear came from the gunhawks as their horses milled furiously, scared by the thunderous sound which had broken the stillness into a thousand screaming fragments of noise. The rifles cracked again, emptying more saddles. One of the men who had led the file through the pass yelled a sharp order. Jeff saw him touch spurs to his mount, leading the pack deeper into the valley, as if the other had suddenly realised that only in that direction lay temporary safety, and a chance to think things out without lead crashing in their direction. Swinging his weapon, Jeff tried to sight on the man, loosed off two shots, but both missed.

Several other men reined their mounts to face into the valley, slapping their gun barrels across their horses' rumps to urge them on. Jeff aimed again, but this time for the horses, knowing that they presented a far easier target to hit in the darkness and on the run.

One of the animals suddenly went down, slumping forward on its knees, throwing its rider. The man, a dimly seen shadow, leapt from its back the instant it stopped, caught his balance instinctively and commenced to run for the nearest clump of bushes. He was halfway towards them when a hand gun cracked from the other side of the valley, pitching him forward on his face where he lay still, the merest blob of dark shadow on the short grass.

By now, those men still immediately below them had commenced firing back, shooting blindly into the rocks, but hoping no doubt that if they fired a sufficient number of shots, some of them were bound to find their mark. A bullet struck one of the rocks within a foot of Jeff's head, went singing shrilly into the distance, scattering a powdering of rock splinters into his face, cutting along his exposed cheek. He winced as pain lanced momentarily through the side of his face, then forced himself to lift his head once more and peer through the sights of his rifle.

More thin stilettos of gunfire splashed through the dimness. The men below were struggling to control their panicking mounts and still keep up their fire. Caught in the terrible ambuscade, they were gradually being whittled down until very few were still in the saddle and only a mere handful were crouched down among the stunted bushes, shooting back at the darkly shadowed slopes.

'We've got 'em finished,' crowed Shedden in an exultant tone. He rammed fresh cartridges into his smoking gun, fired again and again, switching targets whenever he saw a man go down. This was how they had fought during the war, Jeff thought fiercely, feeling the strange tingle race along his nerves and limbs. A hit and run type of fight against a vastly superior enemy, cutting him down to size. Guerilla tactics which had proved to be so successful when battling the Yankee columns in the thickets of the wilderness. Now it was the war all over again and even as the thought flashed through his mind, he wondered sharply if those three men were down there, if any of them had been killed in their withering hail of lead. It seemed more than likely and as the return fire from below diminished, he began to crawl towards the far end of the ledge, intending to go down and take a closer look for himself.

As if divining his reason, Fenner laid a hand on his arm. 'You're goin' to look for those three men you're huntin'?' he said. There was only a faintly questioning tone to his voice.

Jeff nodded his head. 'If they are there, then I want them to know who engineered this ambush. If they aren't then I want to know so that I can go out to the Triple Bar ranch and finish what I came here for.'

For a second, the other's grip tightened on his arm as though to restrain him, then it fell away as if the other had realised that such restraint would be useless anyway.

'Those down there won't last very long,' acknowledged the other. 'But I'm just a trifle worried about that bunch who rode deeper into the valley. They could have been making for the homesteads and if they do, they might get Susan and decide to hold her hostage.'

Jeff sucked in a sharp intake of air. It was something he had not previously considered and he cursed himself savagely for not having realised it. Of course, that was exactly what those men would do. They would have realised who and why this ambush had been set up, would have known that the girl would not be with them. Picking his way along the ledge, he reached his horse a few minutes later, swung up into the saddle and started down-grade.

CHAPTER 6

MAN WITH A GUN

The two small homesteads lay deathly hushed in the moonlight. Jeff rode straight for the further of them, slid from the saddle instinctively as he spotted the three horses a little way to the right of the small hay barn. It was a move which undoubtedly saved his life for at that precise moment there came a splash of flame, lashing from the darkness near the barn and a bullet hummed viciously through the air where his head had been a moment earlier. Dropping on to his hands and knees, he scurried towards the squared shadows that lay in the small court-yard, straining for a shifting silhouette which would give away the position of at least one of the trio of gunmen. When it came, it was from one of the horses, moving around in the short grass just beyond the patch of recently cultivated earth with an uneasiness that any born range man instantly understood. One of the gunmen was moving around close to that horse, spooking it.

Crawling forward, careful not to lift his head, he reached the small trough that stood at one side of the yard and pressed himself down into the dirt behind it, glancing cautiously around the end. An indistinct shape showed in the gloom at the edge of the barn. It was moving slowly and with evident difficulty in the direction of the house. There was also the faintly heard scuff of cloth in the dust and he knew instinctively that the other had been wounded. That still left two men unaccounted for.

Jeff eased his way softly forward, straining to make out either of the other two gunmen, but seeing nothing in the long shadows. Then there came the sharp sound of metal striking wood, the frightened snicker of the horse and, as though knowing that this sound had betrayed him, the wounded gunhawk began firing swiftly and recklessly into the darkness, the long stiletto of flame blooming in stabbing, flashes of light.

At the same instant, gunfire came from a different direction. One of the other men, holed up by the house, loosed off several shots, all of them striking wide of Jeff's position. Propping himself up on one elbow, he fired at the two sources of gunfire, heard the wounded man utter a loud sigh that trailed off into utter silence.

Swinging, he fired again at the man near the house, saw the other move out, scuttle across a patch of open ground where the flooding yellow moonlight picked out his shape for a brief moment. Jeff's hand did not attempt to follow the other. Even before he could do so there came a sharp, unmistakable report of a rifle from one of the side windows of the house and the moving silhouette suddenly jerked, stiffened, and then slithered forward for a couple of feet before lying still, arms and legs sprawled out in the moonlight.

Scanning the deceptive overtones of shadow that lay thick and huge around the small homestead, Jeff called softly forward: 'Keep back from the windows, Susan. There's still another critter around.'

He saw the pale blur of the girl's face move, disappear from the square opening of the window. The stink of burnt powder came to him out of the clinging stillness as he searched with eyes and ears, straining every sense to pick out the third man he knew to be hiding somewhere close by, waiting his time to strike.

Cautiously, Jeff went forward, crouching low to present a more difficult target. Total silence had closed down, except for the faint rattle of gunfire in the distance where the rest of the men were finishing off the gunhawks who were trying to get away through the pass and out into the desert. Jeff reckoned that very few of them would be successful and although Marsden probably had the same number of men back at the Triple Bar ranch, things would have evened their respective forces up tremendously during the evening.

He found the three horses standing patiently, their reins looped over one of the wooden posts at the edge of the compound. The man he had killed lay on his face close to one of the animals. Turning him over, Jeff felt the unmistakable limpness, let the other's arm fall to the dirt and crawled on, circling around the house. The third man was not at the rear of the house where Jeff had half-expected to find him. Knitting his brows, he tried to figure out where he would go in these circumstances and was on the point of continuing his wary advance when he heard the faint sound that came from inside the house.

It was a muffled sound, almost as though someone had tried to make a cry for help only to have it cut off before it could be uttered, as if a rough hand had been clapped over someone's mouth before they really had a chance to scream.

Susan! The thought pounded through his brain even as he thrust himself to his feet and launched himself forward across the stretch of open space, caring little for his own safety, knowing that by doing this he was exposing himself to gunfire from one of the windows. Reaching the rear door, he found it slightly ajar. Carefully, making no sound, he pushed it open, slid inside and pressed himself tightly against the wall, straining to pick out the slightest sound.

So far, he had made no attempt to yell, to warn the girl that he had heard her and was coming. The last thing he wanted to do was to give the other any indication that he was inside the house, knowing how easy it would be for the gunhawk to kill the girl, or use her as a human shield to make his escape. So long as the gunslinger was not aware of his presence there, he might have a chance to take him by surprise.

He felt his way along the dark passage, came to the door which led into the small bedroom where the girl had been crouched at the window. Holding his breath until it hurt in his lungs, he listened intently. At first, he could hear nothing beyond the thumping of his blood through his veins. Then he fancied he heard the faint sound of breathing inside the room. A moment later, he was certain.

What was happening inside the room? Where was the girl, and the killer? Was he peering intently out of the window, waiting for him to show himself out there in the dusty moonlit courtyard? Had he got his gun pressed into the girl's back, ready to pull the trigger and squeeze off the shot which would snap her spine in a single second of time? A host of half-formed thoughts and possibilities raced riotously through Jeff's mind as he stood there at the door, trying to make up his mind on his best course of action. If only it was possible to create some form of diversion, to pull the other's attention away from the girl, just for the few seconds he would need.

A moment later, the silence was blown apart by the thunderous lash of gunfire emanating from inside the room, the echoes roaring in Jeff's ears in the confined space. Drawing back his leg, he was on the point of kicking the door open and going inside, when he heard on the atrophying echoes of that single gunshot, the faint beat of hoofs outside the building. From inside the room, a man's harsh voice yelled: 'Hold it right there, mister, if you want your daughter to stay alive. Call off that other *hombre* who's roamin' around outside. Have him move into the courtyard where I can see him, with his hands lifted over his head where I can see 'em, or the next bullet goes into her back. You got that, Fenner?'

Jeff sucked in a soundless gust of air. So Fenner had ridden up to see what was happening here. Gently, he pushed open the door, careful not to make a sound.

'Better hurry, Fenner, and get that *hombre* where I can see him. My patience is wearin' a trifle thin."

Dimly, he heard Fenner call: 'I don't know where he is. That's the truth. I—'

Jeff could afford to wait no longer. There was the chance that the gunman would shoot the girl and then fight it out with the others. Through the crack in the door, he was just able to make out the dark figure of the man standing close by the window, peering out into the night. The girl was in one corner, her rifle lying on the floor at the gunman's feet. He could just make out the pale, grey blur of her face.

'Drop that gun,' Jeff called quietly.

There was a slow stiffening of the other's body from the shoulders down to the waist, a tensing of the muscles. His mind would be working fast now, knowing that Jeff had got the drop on him and that if he was to get out of this mess, he would have to think and act fast. He did not obey Jeff's order, still kept a tight hold on the gun. Now that he was able to see him a little more clearly, even though the other's face was only partially in profile, Jeff realised that there was something strangely familiar about him.

'You goin' to drop that iron, or do I have to drop you?'

'You wouldn't do that,' the other said. 'You ain't the type.'

Now that he came to listen more carefully to the man's voice, Jeff realised who it was. This was Ed Denson, one of the three men he had been trailing. He felt the sudden tightening of the muscles of his chest and stomach as they knotted themselves painfully and his finger jerked a little, spasmodically, on the trigger. Very softly, he said: 'You ought to know better than that, Denson. I swore to trail you and kill you as soon as I caught up with you, for what you did back in the war. Or maybe you figured I'd forgotten about that.'

Still there was no attempt on the gunman's part to drop the gun he held in his hand, nor did he make any move to turn. 'So you are Jeff Denver,' said the other after a brief pause. 'I had the feelin' that you might be when we got word as to what happened to Cranshield. Only a man as fast as you could've beaten him to the draw, even though there were those who said you'd shot him down from the back.'

'Only now you know better, don't you?'

'Sure.' The other's tone took on a sudden whining note. 'Listen, Denver. Suppose we discuss this real peaceable like. Ain't no reason why we should kill each other, is there? You had your job to do durin' the war, and I had mine. We both did it accordin' to our lights. Nothin' wrong in that, was there? Everythin' is fair in love and war, you know.'

'I'm goin' to kill you, Denson,' grated Jeff tightly. 'Nothin' you say is goin' to alter the fact.'

'And if I refuse to draw against you? What then? You intend to shoot me in the back?' Denson gave a faint shake of his head. 'I know you a lot better than that, Denver. You're the honourable type who always gives his opponent the chance to go for his gun.'

'You're forgettin' those fifty men who died because of you. You're forgettin' that any honour I had went when they court-martialled me and imprisoned me. I've got no pity for you, Denson. You're not worth the dust under my feet.'

'I'm still not goin' to turn and face you, I'm just goin'

to—' Even before he had finished speaking, the other spun swiftly on his heel. His talk had all been to take Jeff off his guard. Almost, it succeeded. The girl's sharp cry of warning initiated a train of reflex actions. Simultaneously with the warning flash in his head, Jeff brought up the barrel of his own gun and squeezed off a single shot. Twin muzzle blast sounded almost together. The shrill echoes ran tumultuously from room to room inside the house, diminishing gradually. As they died away, there seemed to be no sound at all in the room, as if it had been sheared off by a machete. Then Denson lurched forward like a drunken man, his fingers spread across his chest, his head lowered a little, a stupid expression on it as he stared down at the red stain which soaked into his shirt and began to dribble between his fingers. His gun slid from his nerveless hand, clattered to the floor in front of him, a moment before his body crashed on top of it.

Scarcely aware of the brief stabs of pain which lanced through his left arm, Jeff went forward, the barrel of his gun laid on the man at his feet, his finger hard on the trigger. Then he thrust the weapon back into its holster. Bending, he propped the dying man up against the wall just beneath the window. There was no look of great suffering on the other's dimly visible features. But there was the indelible shadow of death written all over his face, in the unnatural brightness of his eyes which seemed to have suddenly become sunk deep into his head, looking out at Jeff, curiously motionless as though not seeing him, but staring at something far beyond him.

'How bad is he?' asked the girl, coming forward and going down on one knee beside Jeff. Her voice was little more than a faint, husky whisper.

'He's finished,' Jeff said quietly; 'and he knows it.'

Denson licked his dry lips, then said throatily, 'The pain seems to have gone now.' He hesitated for a moment and then, with an effort, lifted his gaze and fixed it on Jeff's face. 'This is the big one, ain't it, Denver?'

'That's right.'

'I suppose I knew it was foolish to try to run from a man like you. But you won't make it. The other two will be on your trail now. They know their only chance of stayin' alive is to make damned sure you're dead. Me – I didn't figure you'd be here, that was my big mistake. But they won't be as stupid as that. They'll get you, Denver.'

'Maybe.' Jeff heard the sound of Fenner coming in at the door. 'But I'm forewarned too. How'd you know they weren't killed with the others near the pass?'

'They weren't ridin' with us on this trip. Still back at the ranch.' The dying man's tone was blurring and thickening inevitably as his throat muscles and tongue failed to respond to his efforts to speak properly. There came the soft, sighing rattle deep in the other's throat, a faint exhalation of air through his half-open lips.

'Denson?' Jeff's voice was soft, inquiring now. He reached out and touched the other's limp arm, felt the coldness and let it go, getting slowly to his feet. Hal Fenner's gaze probed his from the other side oft the room. 'He's dead?' asked the older man.

'He's dead,' Jeff affirmed. 'He was one of the men I came to kill.'

'I gathered that from what he said before he died.' The other's tone lacked emotion. 'We got most of the other gunhawks at the pass. Half a dozen or so managed to break out and across the desert. Most of them was wounded bad and we saw no hope of catchin' up with 'em at night, so we let 'em go. In spite of that, this was a good night's work. I figure it's shown Marsden that we sure mean business out here. He'll think twice before sendin' his boys to burn us out.'

'What are we going to do with him?' asked Susan Fenner, pointing to the dead gunman on the floor.

'I'll get some of the others to take him out and bury

him along with the rest,' said her father briskly. He moved towards the door, then turned and gave Jeff a bright-sharp glance, faintly appraising.

'What do you aim to do now, Jeff? Stick around here or go out to the Triple Bar and try to find those other two men, force a fight with them?'

'I guess that's it as far as I'm concerned. My business here is only half finished. As for the rest of you, I'd walk warily, even now. You may think that you've bested Marsden and he'll be forced to recognise your rights to this land, but don't underestimate him. He's a determined man and he still has the money to bring in more gunmen from the hills and gather some of the desert crowd to him. If he does that, you may find that you're right back where you started, facing a much superior force. All you'll have gained, will be a little breathin' space. If you want my advice, for what it's worth, spend that time wisely. Be sure that you're ready for him if he rides against you again.'

'There could be a lot of truth in what you say,' muttered the other musingly. He paused for a moment, then turned on his heel sharply. 'I'll get some of the others to bury these men. I doubt if Marsden will send any of his men against us tonight.'

Kneeling, Jeff Denver looked down through the pine branches on to the wide cart road that ran in a wide sweep to the Triple Bar ranch some four hundred yards away. In the grey light of dawn, he sat in the saddle and made himself a smoke, patient and able to bide his time. There were a dozen or so horses in the corral which fronted the imposing building and he guessed that most of Marsden's force was still there and the single yellow light that shone in the window looking out over the wide courtyard was mute testimony to the fact that one man, at least, was still awake, unable to sleep. He figured that this man was Cal Marsden. Sooner or later, the other was going to have to make a move or concede defeat to the squatters, and when he did, Jeff was anxious to be ready to move in.

He freed himself of his speculations; at this juncture they were not pertinent to the job in hand. Lighting his cigarette, he sat forward, arms crossed on the pommel, relishing the taste of the cigarette on his tongue. A few moments later, he heard a faint sound off in the distance, in the direction of Culver Creek, a sound which grew louder as it approached. Five minutes later he could hear the protesting creak of leather and the labouring sounds of a pair of horses, knew that it was a wagon moving out to the Triple Bar place. He drew his horse a little further back into the dim shadow of the pines and scanned the dark road. Now he could make out the shape of the wagon less than a hundred yards away and the solitary figure driving it. The man moved the team slowly as though reluctant to continue this journey and as he drew level with Jeff, the other saw that it was the doctor from Culver Creek. The doctor let his team have their heads as they went down the slope among the pines and soon they came out into the open ground and moved into the dusty court-yard. Jeff watched closely as the other climbed down, took up his bag and moved towards the house. When the door opened, his tall gaunt figure was outlined against the beam of yellow lamplight which flooded out. He went inside and the door closed behind him. Come to treat some of the wounded who had managed to straggle back after their punishing defeat.

Inside the parlour of the ranch-house, Cal Marsden faced Doc Flynn with a look of tightly-controlled anger on his broad features. Judging from the haggard expression, Flynn guessed that the other had been awake all night, reckoned that something had to be very wrong for this to have happened, and wondered what could have occurred to put the rancher in this mood.

'I got you out here to tend to some of my men, Flynn,'

Marsden told him harshly. 'There was a little trouble and they got shot up pretty badly.'

'Trouble?' inquired the other mildly. He set his bag down on the table. 'What sort of trouble? I heard nothing about it in town.'

'You wouldn't,' said the other tightly. 'It happened out near the valley where those damned nesters have stolen my land. They rustled part of my herd off the range, drove it into the valley and then trapped my men inside, cutting them down before they had a chance to ride out.'

Flynn, who had no real liking for Marsden merely grunted at the news, then said: 'Where are these men of yours? Let me take a look at them and then get back into town. I'm not used to bein' called out here to tend men like these in the middle of the night.'

Marsden lit a thin, black cheroot, blew smoke into the air. 'I didn't ask you out to give me no goddamned lecture, Flynn. Just you do your job and have less to say about it. I can make things really hot for you back in town if I ever have a mind to – and don't you ever forget that.'

'I'm not forgetting anything,' said Flynn mildly. 'Only remember that it won't be easy for you to get another doctor to work in Culver Creek.'

'You'll stay,' said Marsden confidently. 'You know which side your bread is buttered.' He fixed a baleful stare on the other, until Flynn looked away, then turned, snatched up his bag from the table and marched to the door.

It was almost an hour later before he had finished and came back into the house. Marsden was in no better mood. He was still seated at the long table, his unshaven features looking more haggard in the first pale rays of sunlight which filtered through the window. There was a half bottle of whisky in front of him and a little left in the glass.

'Well?' he snapped. He tossed back the remainder of the liquor in the glass.

'They'll all live – unfortunately.'

'Don't try my patience too far, Flynn. I assure you that I'm not in the mood for it.'

'Seems to me, from what some of those hired killers of yours were saying that you're in more trouble than you care to admit, even to yourself. Half of your private army of gunslingers dead or wounded, and the nesters growing stronger and more numerous every week as more wagon trains move in. There is talk in town that a big train is moving out this way right now.'

'I'm not interested in what the town gossips say.' Marsden poured more whisky into the glass, spilling some on to the top of the polished table as his hand shook a little.

Flynn shrugged nonchalantly. 'Could be that you'd be well advised to listen. You've been the kingpin here merely because you've been able to terrorise everyone in the territory. But that time is passing – and fast.'

'I can always bring in more gunhawks if I have need of 'em,' sneered the other harshly. 'There are plenty of men who will sell their guns to me for the right price.'

'I think you would at that,' grunted the doctor. He moved towards the door. 'Bloodshed means nothing to you, just as long as you get your own way.' He paused, then said tightly: 'Can I leave now?'

'Get out of my sight,' muttered Marsden. He sank deeper into gloom after the other had gone, staring straight in front of him, feeling the deep-seated anger grow in his mind. He put all of his recent troubles squarely at the door of this stranger who had ridden into Culver Creek – Denver. If only Cranshield had carried out his job properly all of this could have been avoided and those troublesome nesters would have been driven from the territory. Once he had made that stand, there would have been little further trouble from them; of that he felt quite certain.

Now his crowd was badly mauled. He had no idea at the moment how many of them would stay with him even if he did manage to hire more men from the desert bands. The majority of these men were outlaws, men on the run from the law, brave men if they were cornered by themselves and knew they had to turn and fight to save their own lives, brave too when they held a superiority in numbers. But now more than half of them had been in that bunch attacked in the valley and they had been defeated. There was no point in denying that, especially to himself. He had the inescapable feeling that they would turn and run with their tails between their legs; they were that kind.

Even if they did stick by him, he knew he would have a hard time keeping his iron control over them. They would have lost some of their confidence in him as a leader, would be wary of going through with any further plans he made. He got to his feet, hunted around in the room for another bottle of whisky, found it and went back to the table. Glancing in the mirror on the far wall, he took a good look at himself. The two-day growth of beard gave him a drawn, haggard look and his eyes were deep-sunk and lacked lustre.

Finishing his drink, he lurched to his feet, went outside to the bunkhouse. Most of the men were up and he noticed the way in which they tried not to meet his glance. They were suspicious, possibly even a little afraid and guilty. He called Brad Foley, the new foreman, over, walked with him to the rail of the corral before speaking.

'I want you to round up as many of the men as you can get, Brad. Take them out to the main herd, keep an eye on it until I decide what to do now. I don't reckon those damned nesters will dare to make another sneak attack like they did last night, but it pays to be careful. Maybe I've made the big mistake of underestimating this bunch in the past; but believe me, it's not goin' to happen again.'

'What if they figure they're big enough to ride out here

114

and attack the ranch?' inquired the other doubtfully. He was a tall spare-framed man. He had not wanted this job as foreman, but it had been thrust on him and he was trying to do it to the best of his ability.

'They won't do that,' said Marsden thinly, striving to make his voice more confident than he felt inwardly. 'Now get the men together and ride out. I'll leave Fossiter here. I'm ridin' into town to have a talk with the sheriff. I figure it might be better if he was to ride out with a posse of townsfolk and serve a warrant on Denver and those nesters.'

From his vantage point among the pines, Jeff watched the sun lift over the lip of the eastern horizon, felt the first warm touch of it on his face, then glanced back towards the ranch-house down below him as a bunch of men made their way out of the bunkhouse and over to the corral, roping in their horses, saddling up, ready to ride out. He screwed up his mouth as he tried to figure out what might lie behind this move. It could be that Marsden had decided to send out his men on a raiding party right away, to burn out the Fenners and the Sheddens. On the other hand, he might be concerned about his herd, had decided to send men out to watch it in case of another attack.

Down below, the men made themselves ready, then rode out of the courtyard, the cloud of dust kicked up by their mounts hanging in the air for several minutes before it finally settled. Jeff had scanned the faces of the men in the party, had seen nothing of Matt Woodrow and Reno Kearney. He began to wonder about those two men. Why had they been left out of that group of riders? It was unlikely that Marsden would have singled them out for a special job. He waited until the sound of the horses had faded into the distance, then moved his mount down trail, through the tall, slender trees, the thickly tangled foliage on either side of the narrow game-run sheltering him from sight.

He stopped still at the very edge of the trail as he caught the sound of another horse in the courtyard. With his hat pulled well down over his eyes, which were narrowed as he searched the area, he saw the man hitching the horse to the wagon that stood in front of the house. It was someone he did not recognise but a few moments later, there was no mistaking the man who came stalking from the house and climbed up into the wagon.

Flicking the whip across the horse's back, Marsden drove out of the courtyard and on to the winding trail as if all the devils in hell were on his tail. Jeff waited until the other had gone by at a storming pace, then eased his mount out on to the trail and walked it in the direction of the ranch.

Passing through the wooden gate, he rode more slowly, sitting tall and straight in the saddle, both caution and interest coming to their sudden peak in him. He brushed the butt of his gun with his fingertips almost absently as he reined up in the middle of the courtyard, the sharp, acrid smell of dust in his nostrils. He did not, for some odd reason which he could not fathom, feel any fear. Stopping quite still, he swung his sharp glance around him. He was holding the reins lightly in his hands when he caught the movement inside the entrance of the barn. A moment later a voice yelled: 'What in tarnation you have to ride back for? Forgotten somethin'? Or did you figure that you'd follow those other two over the hill?'

Sliding from the saddle now that he knew where the other man was, Jeff went easily forward, coming up behind the other. The man was busily forking hay into a pile in the centre of the barn floor, did not turn as Jeff approached, but said in a testy tone, 'Cat got your tongue?'

When Jeff still did not answer, suspicion ticked at the other and he spun quickly into a rigid, peering posture, putting up one hand to sweep back his hat so that he could see more clearly in the stable's gloom.

''Say, you ain't—' Even as the shock of realisation came to him, the other went for his gun, then froze into a rigid position, fingers spread but not quite touching the butt of the gun at his waist. His eyes had widened as he saw the speed of Jeff's draw and he stared as though mesmerised at the dark hole in the barrel of the Colt which was now pointed, unmoving at his stomach.

'That's right,' Jeff said softly. 'Just hold it right there. I don't want to have to kill you, but I mean to have the answers to some questions before I ride back out of here, and you're the one to give me them.'

The other stepped back a pace, moved his right hand well clear of his gun. His eyes narrowed in brief speculation. 'What'd you want to know, mister?'

'Your name for a start.'

'Clem Fossiter. I work here for Marsden.'

'I'm Jeff Denver. Could be that you've heard Marsden talk of me?' He saw, at once, by the look on the other's face that the name meant quite a lot to him.

'Denver.' The word was an explosive hiss. 'You're the *hombre* who led those nesters last night, who shot up most of the boys.'

Fossiter, Jeff figured, was more on edge than he had expected. It was something more than the surprised fear he would have anticipated from the other just being told his name.

'Somethin' seems to be troublin' you, Fossiter,' Jeff told the other mildly. 'You got somethin' on your mind?'

'Trouble? Nothin' like that. Just that I never figured you'd be fool enough to ride into this place like this. There are more'n a score of men in the bunkhouse and—'

Jeff shook his head slowly. 'You don't fool me for a minute, Fossiter. I saw them ride out less than half an hour ago – and Marsden left just before I rode in. My guess is that you're alone here and you're scared. You don't know

117

what I'm goin' to do to you.'

'Now listen,' broke in the other hurriedly. 'I just work for Marsden. I get the orders and I do as I'm told. I ain't one of those hired gunhawks you saw ride out a while ago. That's why Marsden left me behind. He knows I'm no use with a gun and—'

'Save all of the talk,' Jeff snapped. 'I'm not interested in you. But I do want two men. Reno Kearney and Matt Woodrow. I know they work for Marsden too, so you don't have to try to lie. And I also know that they didn't ride out with the rest of the men.'

'They did work for Marsden, Denver. But not any more.'

'What do you mean by that?' Jeff's voice was harsh, more strident than before.

'Just that they rode out a couple of hours ago. Took what wages was due to them and headed over the hill. My guess is they won't stop ridin' until they get clear to California.'

'What made 'em pull out like that? Some quarrel with Marsden?'

The other shook his head slyly. 'More likely they heard what happened to the third *hombre* who came with 'em when they applied for this job.'

'You meanin' Denson?'

'That's the one. Guess you know what happened to him, more'n anybody else.'

Reaching out, Jeff grabbed the other by the arm, his grip tightening savagely. 'You're sure about this, Fossiter? You ain't tellin' me this because they asked you to, just to throw me off their trail?'

Fossiter twisted, grimacing, struggling to break free but Jeff's fingers tightened powerfully.

'Let go my arm, dammit,' hissed the other, his breath gushing from his lips as he winced with agony. 'You'll break it.'

'Answer my question.'

'Hell, I'm tellin' you the truth. They just upped and rode out, soon as they heard from the others what had happened. Maybe they're scared you'll do the same to them if you ever catch up with them.'

'I'll catch up with them all right.' Jeff's arm fell slowly away. He continued to regard Fossiter through a moment of half-believing stillness. Then he took the other's Colt from his holster and tossed it out through the barn door where it landed with a dull thud in the dust at the edge of the corral.

Walking swiftly, he went back to his horse, mounted up. Fossiter stood just inside the barn, massaging his arm slowly, lips thinned. Then Jeff wheeled his mount, hauling sharply on the reins, not giving any further backward glance at the other. He had no knowledge of where he would strike the trail which the two men had taken, but he was unwilling to waste any more time asking Fossiter. Even now, the other might be regretting that he had told as much as he had.

The trail from the Triple Bar ranch struck almost due west, climbing through some of the roughest country he had ever known as soon as he left the western boundary wire and headed out across the low foothills which bordered the higher and more rugged mountains.

Of one thing he was quite sure. Those two men would stick together now until they were absolutely convinced that he was not following them. Together, they would figure that they had a chance to defeat him if he did succeed in catching up with them. Separated, they could be taken one at a time. He cut their trail just as the sun was lifting towards its zenith, the shimmering, burning waves of heat beating down on his body, bringing all of the moisture out to the surface, oozing though his pores until he was soaked with it. The trail was visible only in places where there was thin topsoil among the stretches of bare, rocky ground and from the prints he found, he knew that both men had been pushing their mounts when they had ridden this way.

Pausing on a long, low outcrop of smooth rock, he cast about him, debating the situation. The hills ran on ahead of him in a long, seemingly endless series of undulating peaks and in places, the trail clung to the steep, precipitous sides, little more than a grey scar just visible against the overall background of sun-hazed rock.

The sun was beginning to lower from the zenith when he struck more rolling swales of ground, an advance indication of more prominent peaks still to come and by the time it was middle-down, still burning in his eyes, the dizzying waves of heat shocking back at him from the rocks on all sides, he topped a rise and came upon a small cluster of weather-aged buildings that clung together in a gravelly hollow as though there was some safety in numbers.

CHAPTER 7

GUNMAN'S TRAIL

Carefully, Jeff loosened his holstered gun, let his right hand rest lightly on the butt as he walked his horse slowly along the trail, eyes alert for any sign of life. Outwardly, the place seemed as though it had been left abandoned many years before, a ghost town that had been mouldering here ever since the last inhabitant had pulled out. But he knew from past experience that things were not always what they seemed to be on the surface; that this was just the sort of place Woodrow and Kearney would pick to lie up and wait for him.

A quick glance told him that most of the buildings were not safe to enter. Sagging roofs and caved-in walls all told their own story of a long-abandoned place. Maybe, at some time in the past, there had been silver or gold in the narrow, swift-rushing streams that raced down the shoulders of the mountains hereabouts, and men had come fired with their dreams of riches, had been forced to leave when their dreams had faded into nothingness. But in spite of this, on either side of the trail, especially where it widened into something more than a narrow cutting through the rocky outcrops, there were buildings which still stood, ravaged by time, but upright, affording good shelter to men on the run, where they would be able to watch the trail in both directions and pick off a man from a couple of hundred yards with a high-powered rifle.

Swinging off the horse, he looped up the reins. There was not a solitary sound to be heard, the utter stillness of the hills pressing down on him from all sides; and there was not that odd feeling in the silence that a man might sense if there were hostile eyes watching him, fingers on triggers waiting to place a slug in his body. Nevertheless, he walked warily along the dusty trail, feet scuffing up tiny clouds of the white alkali. It stung the back of his throat and burned in his mouth and nostrils.

The faint whisper of his footsteps echoed back at him from the silent wooden buildings. A sagging boardwalk linked four of them and halfway along the trail which ran down the centre of the ghost town, a taller building which could have been an hotel of some kind, or a saloon, stood derelict. Tumbleweed bowled along the narrow alley that ran alongside the two-storeyed building, rustled against the walls. He looped the reins over the canted hitching rail, stepped cautiously on to the boardwalk. The wooden slats creaked ominously under his weight, but held him as he approached the doors. They hung lop-sidedly on rusted broken hinges, squealed as he thrust them open and stepped into the gloomy stillness of what had once been a bar.

A cracked and blackened mirror hung at the back of the counter and there were still some bottles on the shelves, covered in dust and cobwebs. Tables stood in a neat line against two of the walls, except for one which was in the middle of the floor directly in front of the bar.

There was a man eating from a bowl at the table, a man whose back was towards Jeff as he entered. Instinctively, Jeff's hand dropped to the butt of his gun, then stayed there as the man turned slowly. Slowly, the man pushed himself to his feet, blinking at Jeff. He was in his sixties,

Jeff reckoned. A grizzled white-haired fellow, his face lined and seamed by the years and long exposure to the elements. He was unarmed as far as Jeff could see and there was no hostility on his face, merely a vague surprise at seeing anybody there.

'You all alone in this place?' Jeff asked.

The man's eyes clung to his with a dead steadiness. Then he nodded slowly. 'That's right, mister.' He glanced at the guns Jeff wore. 'You're the third *hombre* to come ridin' through here. First time anyone's been along this trail for close on six months.'

'How long ago were they here?'

'Four, maybe five hours ago,' muttered the other without letting his eyes stray. His lips opened in a leering grin. 'You ridin' after 'em?'

'What makes you think that?' Jeff moved forward until he stood close to the other.

'Easy. Men don't take this trail unless they're on the run from somethin'. And those other two *hombres* sure looked as if they were high-tailin' it out of the territory as fast as their broncs would carry 'em. I figured there'd be another man ridin' this way. Now you turn up. Don't take a blind man to see the connection.'

'And what are you doin' here?' Jeff asked.

'Mindin' my own business.' There was a note of defiance in the others' tone.

Jeff shrugged. 'It's as good a reason as any, I suppose.' He had already tagged the other as somebody who had been on the run for a long while and had found this place of sanctuary and intended staying here as long as possible. If the law should ever ride out here there were so many places where a man could hide, particularly if he knew the place well, as this man undoubtedly did, and for a fugitive, it was the ideal place to stay. He doubted if there was any danger from the other. What went on outside of this town held no concern for him. All he asked was to be left in peace.

He turned, began to move back towards the door, still anxious to be on his way now that he knew himself to be so close.

'Want a drink and a bite to eat?' asked the other, pointing to the table. 'I've got plenty here. Coffee or whisky, so long as you don't mind it a few years old.'

Jeff hesitated, then turned back. 'A drink of coffee is all I've got time for. Then I'll have to be on my way again.'

'Hell, why be in such an all-fired hurry? So you're after those two men. They won't make good time along that trail.'

'How can you be so sure of that?' Jeff seated himself at the table as the other went back to the counter, returned with a cup and set it down in front of him, filling it with hot coffee from the can on the table.

The other rubbed a sleeve over his lips. 'Rode out that way myself a couple of days back. There's been a slide about five miles up into the hills. They'll spend at least two, three, hours, trying to work their way around it. It's a new slide, not packed in yet and there ain't no way they can go around it. They have to stick to the trail. Even when they get around it, they'll have to stay with this trail all the way over the hills. You won't have any trouble tailin' 'em from here.'

Jeff relaxed a little. There were the gnawing pangs of hunger in the bottom of his stomach, but he had decided not to eat until he had sighted the two men. Now, in view of what this man said, he guessed there would be time for him to eat. He took down the hot coffee in noisy swallows. It burned his throat on the way down, but it tasted good, acted as a stimulant.

The other went back to the counter, opened a flap and went through. Turning, Jeff watched him suspiciously for a moment and the other, as if feeling Jeff's gaze on him said: 'I've got a stove through here where I do all my cookin'.' He went into the room at the back and Jeff sat back in his chair, staring straight ahead of him, seeing nothing, grateful for the rest and the chance to do a little thinking. It occurred to him that Kearney and Woodrow would guess he would meet up with this *hombre* and that the other would tell him as much as he knew. So for all he knew, there might be a couple of cocked guns waiting out there for him, somewhere along the trail, perhaps before he reached the slide the other had spoken of.

Sooner or later, he would get all he wanted; an even chance at the two men he had sworn to kill. It was an obligation which had been placed on him that moment when most of his party had been wiped out in that cunningly-laid ambush, so many years before. He rubbed a hand down the side of his face. The memory of it brought back the bitter, angry ache in his body once again, tightening his grip on the edge of the table, knuckles standing out whitely under the taut flesh. When will the memory fade, he wondered tightly? When will there come a time when it ceases to have this effect on me? The old hatred came up inside him again and he could taste the bitterness in his mouth, the old savage desire to face those two traitors at the end of his gun, to destroy them both utterly, to wipe out the stain on his past, on his honour.

But was that all there was to it, he wondered idly? Or was there something more, something he could not even define himself? Those men in his party were dead and nothing could bring them back again. As for his own honour, that had gone at his court-martial. He could never retrieve that no matter how hard he tried.

He sat up in his chair, the smell of frying bacon bringing a sharp pain to his jaw. Ridden hard by his feelings, he brought his fists together, fingers clenched. The other came back with a plate heaped high with bacon and beans. He set it down in front of Jeff.

'Plenty more if you feel like it,' he said genially. Jeff pulled out his pocket knife and set to work, spearing the pieces of bacon with the blade, scooping up the beans on the piece of corn which Jeff guessed the other had baked himself. The oldster watched him with a faintly amused expression on his face.

'Been a long time since I was that hungry,' he observed. 'I found this place more'n three years ago. Lived here ever since. Got everythin' I need. The law never comes this way; only men on the run or those followin' the vengeance trail like yourself. What did those two *hombres* do for you to want to kill 'em so bad?'

'It's a long story,' Jeff said between mouthfuls.

'I got plenty of time, and like I said, you'll catch up with 'em soon enough.'

'All right.' Briefly, Jeff recounted what had happened on that morning in the tangled Wilderness, when he had moved up against the enemy, only to walk straight into an ambush. He told of his court-martial, of how he had discovered that the three men who had acted as scouts had been getting money from the Yankees for their part in leading him into the enemy trap.

The other did not speak until he had finished, then he nodded his head very slowly. 'I guess I know how you feel. It's a long time to carry a grudge, but you got every right to kill these men far as I can see. They looked to be really dangerous killers.'

'Yeah, they are.'

'Maybe you could use help. This place gets unexcitin' now after bein' here for so long and I can still handle a rifle. Besides, I know these hills better than most. There are trails here that only I know, trails through the rocks that could bring you out ahead of these critters.'

Jeff hesitated but only for a moment. 'Thanks anyway,' he said shaking his head. 'But this is somethin' I have to do myself. This is my chore and I want nobody else in it.'

'Don't forget there are two of them,' offered the other. 'They could jump you anywhere along the trail, take you from both sides and you'd never have a chance. You sure you don't want me along?' He glanced up at Jeff hopefully.

'Quite sure, old-timer.' Jeff wiped his plate clean with the last of the bread, poured out a second cup of coffee and sat back, relaxing, building himself a cigarette. He offered the tobacco to the other, then put it back into his pocket at the man's shake of his head. Lighting the cigarette, he blew smoke into the air, regarded the other closely.

'Why don't you get out of here while you still have the chance? You could find yourself some place where you ain't known, wait for the smell of gunsmoke to wear off. Then you'd be free to ride where you like, to sit with your back to the door of a saloon without wonderin' who the next man to come in might be.'

'I thought of that sometime back,' muttered the other, getting to his feet. 'But a man can never go back and cover the same piece of trail twice. Make one mistake, big or small, and it's with you for the rest of your life. No way at all of going back to wipe it out and start afresh.'

'What started you off on the wrong trail?'

'I rode with Quantrill. Most of us were killed, or sent to prison after the war, but I slipped south, just managed to keep one jump ahead of the authorities until I rode out this way, intendin' to make it over the hills and came across this abandoned place. Maybe I was luckier than most, maybe not. Could be that those who died were the fortunate ones. Not those who were left behind.'

'I still figure that you'd be better off ridin' out of here. But not with me. This is too much like what you did before.'

Finishing his smoke, he ground it out under his boot, then scraped back his chair and got to his feet. 'Thanks for the meal and the drink. Now I reckon I'd better be on my way if I'm to reach that slide before dark. I don't relish the idea of tryin' to work my way around it after sundown.'

127

'You sure you don't want me along?' There was a note of pleading in the other's voice.

Jeff laid a hand on the other's arm. 'Just think on what I've said; ride on out of here, but the other way to that I'm goin' and keep on ridin' until you're far enough from here that nobody knows you.'

He went outside, into the dusty, windblown street. Tumbleweed scudded around his legs as he walked to his horse. The faint, whining sound of the wind reached his ears and by now the sun was dipping swiftly to the west, just showing over a rim of rock that stood out black and in stark silhouette against the red sunlight that streamed down into the valley some two hundred feet below.

Swinging up into the saddle, he held the reins loosely in his hands, glanced back to where the oldster stood in the doorway of the decrepit saloon, peering out at him, hands shading his eyes from the sunlight.

'There's a plank bridge over the river about three miles from here,' called the other harshly. 'The slide is half a mile further on.'

'Thanks.' Jeff raised his hand in salute, then touched spurs to his horse and rode out of the ghost town, turned a sharp corner and put the place behind him. The high shoulders of the mountains began to crowd down on him from both sides, rearing up into the bright, blue heavens. He kept his eyes on the stunted trees and rocks that lined the narrow trail. There was not a sign of life anywhere that he could see and somehow, it occurred to him that since they had lit out fast from the Triple Bar ranch, heading west, Kearney and Woodrow would keep on riding as fast and as far as they could, hoping to get a good lead on him. It was possible that the old man back in that ghost town had recognised them for the type of men they were – he had said he had been expecting someone to come riding in after them – and had not mentioned the slide which had virtually blocked the trail. If that were so, then there would have been no reason for those two men to believe they could not keep riding all day, putting several miles between him and themselves before nightfall. Not until they hit the obstruction would they start to think about keeping a watch on the trail behind them until they had found a way around the slide.

Half an hour later, he heard the muted thunder of the river in the distance and slowed his horse to a walk. The slide lay half a mile beyond the river and this obstacle could be the spot where they were waiting for him. The shadows came, lying across the trail as he approached the bridge which lay around a bend in the trail. Everything turned blue. After the strong sunlight, the brilliant reds and golds of evening, after the heat of the day, it was a new world that lay about him; a still, quiet world of dimness and coolness.

The river tumbled its thunderous, brawling length down the side of the mountain, crashing in a sea of foam and spray a quarter of a mile from the wooden bridge. There was a clinging mist in the air, a dampness that Jeff could feel as he rode slowly, cautiously forward. In a few yards of progress, he reached the end of the bridge, paused for a moment, eyeing the far side with a speculative glance, running his gaze along the bank, searching for any sign of movement.

When he saw nothing, he gigged his mount across the bridge, the hollow echo of its hooves preceding him to the other side. By now it was deep twilight and he could not see far. Anyone could hide among the gloomy under-growth, less than a couple of feet from the trail and be sure of not being seen. He fully expected to feel the crash of a bullet in him as he put his horse to the upgrade.

The light was dying out by the time he swung around a bend in the trail, rode between two high rocks that stood like gaunt, silent sentinels on either side, then saw the dull shadow of the slide where it lay over the trail. He halted his mount some distance away, slid smoothly from the saddle and went down on one knee. Less than a minute later, he found the tracks of two horses in the loose, friable soil and he judged from the way the edges of the prints still crumbled, that they had been made less than a couple of hours before.

Getting to his feet, he peered forward, pushing his sight through the clinging gloom, trying to make out details of the terrain which lay in front of him. The trail, in places, pitched steeply for several yards before levelling off again, and in other places where it clung to the side of the cliff, it was less than a couple of feet in width so that he was forced to advance slowly, an inch at a time, pressing his body in to the rough rocks.

As the oldster back in that deserted township had said, it was a comparatively new slide, the earth not yet packed firmly, and in places the entire face of the rock seemed to have been torn away by the avalanche of dirt and rocks which had cascaded down the steep slope, tearing away vegetation and outcrops, half-burying the trail in its debris. Bending, he traced the tracks of the two horses all the way forward until his outstretched fingers encountered the dirt, digging into it and heaving a little off the ledge to his right. He heard the small stones bounce and rattle down the slope for a long way before they came to rest at the bottom and he guessed that he was quite a way up the side of the cliff. Too far if he made one wrong move and went over the edge in the darkness. The horse, too, was wary and a little doubtful of what it was heading into. It tried to stop frequently, hauling hard on the reins as Jeff pulled it forward after him, easing it along with soft, soothing words to allay its natural fears. The last thing he wanted now would be for the horse to panic. On a trail as narrow as this, he doubted if he could calm it down sufficiently to prevent it from going over the edge.

The tracks he was following moved away from the cliff

wall, out to the edge of the trail and he soon came upon a spot where the earth had been shovelled over the side, clearing the trail for perhaps a foot and a half. It was a difficult enough passage in broad daylight when he judged those two had moved along it, but in pitch blackness, with no moonlight filtering down this side of the trail, it would be plain suicide. He debated whether or not to rest up for the remainder of the night, to go forward in the morning when he would be able to see what he was doing, but even as the idea crossed his mind, he instantly rejected it. He had come too far, had been through too much, to ease off now. The grim determination to see this through, to bring it to an end, was the one, overriding thought in his mind, the one thing which drove him on, occupying his thoughts virtually to the exclusion of everything else. Risking a light, he struck a match and peered closely at the ground. In the pale orange glow he was able to make out the prints of the two horses more clearly now and here there were also the footprints of the men, leading their animals forward, edging around the slide, moving very close to the lip of the ridge.

Gingerly, he led the horse forward. It was a good animal, a thoroughbred, but even so, it jibbed occasionally as its feet slipped on the treacherous surface and it took him the best part of an hour to clear the obstacle. Getting to the other side, he continued to press himself against the cliff side until he was sure there were no further slides. His body felt bruised and bleeding, arms and legs raw from the continual scraping from the rough rocks which thrust themselves out at him from the steep wall and underfoot. Standing quite still for a long moment, he sucked air down into his aching lungs, gathering his strength. Cold wind scoured down the valley here where it had narrowed until it formed a natural funnel, channelling the wind along it.

Bending, he tightened the cinch under the thoroughbred's belly. His face was hot and sticky with sweat and his shirt clung to his back, chafing with every movement he made.

Leading the horse forward a little way, he still took his steps with caution, realising that he could see very little in the darkness, that very soon he would be forced to rest up for the night. Whatever happened, he did not want to run into those two men if they had made camp somewhere along the trail and get ahead of them without being aware of it.

Hunger gnawed at his belly and his throat felt parched and dry. There was a deep-seated weariness in his bones that made every movement an agony and when he came to a place where the trail moved in from the precipice, through tall pines which blocked off much of the wind, he paused, scouted around the place until he had satisfied himself that there was no danger there, and hobbled his mount at the edge of a small clearing. He did not dare risk a fire and made cold camp, shivering in his blankets as the sweat congealed on his body. There was a continuing ache in his limbs, but his weariness was enough to make him forget the pain and he was almost instantly asleep.

Twenty minutes after Jeff had hauled his horse off the trail and into the small clearing, Woodrow and Kearney halted their mounts on a wide, smooth outcrop of rock overlooking a small tributary of the river. Although it was still dark here, the moon had risen and they were now around the massive shoulder of the mountain, so that there was light enough to see by, but not enough to be sure of everything they saw.

Kearney rubbed a leg where their encounter with the landslide had chafed the flesh raw. There was the warm stickiness of blood on his fingers when he lifted them away from his thigh.

'We got to rest up sometime, Matt. Ain't no sense tryin' to ride this trail durin' the night. Too many places where

132

a man can go over the edge if he ain't careful. It'll be a bad trail in broad daylight, but we've got no chance at all durin' the night.'

'You'll have even less chance if Denver catches up with us. If that happens, I guess you know what he'll do. I don't care to go up against him unless I've got the pickin' of the time and the spot.'

'Denver's no fool. If he is on our trail, he won't risk movin' past that slide after dark.'

'You reckon not.' There was doubt in Woodrow's voice as he turned his head to survey their surroundings. 'We don't know how close he is to us. He could still be back in Culver Creek fightin' for those nesters , or he could have moved past the slide before it got full dark and be less than a quarter of a mile away.'

Kearney shook his head. 'You're too goddamned jumpy. He hasn't even discovered that we've pulled out from the Triple Bar ranch. Now let's get some rest.' He got down from his horse and led it forward, deeper into the stunted trees.

Woodrow sat quite still in the saddle for a long moment, straining every sense to pick up the sound of pursuit. But there were only the normal night sounds and finally he got down too and followed Kearney.

They made cold camp too, eating stringy jerky beef and washing it down with water from the stream. Before first light, Woodrow was up, moving to the edge of the clearing where the trees thinned and he was able to look back along the trail which he and Kearney had ridden the previous night. In the daylight it looked different to what he had imagined it to be. He could just make out the dark scar of the slide, standing out against the grey-green background of rock and thin vegetation. There was no sign of any rider on that stretch of the trail, no small cloud of dust that would indicate a horse moving towards them and he relaxed with an effort.

Kearney pushed himself to his feet, pulled a strip of jerky from his pack and thrust it into his mouth, chewing on it reflectively. 'Like I told you he's nowhere within miles of us. Likely it'll be days before he decides to go lookin' for us at Marsden's place and when he does, it'll be too late for him to have any hope of catchin' us before we get clear to the Californian border.'

'Maybe you're right at that,' the other acknowledged. He bit off a piece of the smoke-cured meat and lapsed into a bleak, stony silence. Inwardly, he was still not quite as convinced of this as Kearney seemed to be. It had occurred to him that if Denver had been trailing them, he would have traced their trail clear to the slide and then pulled off the road into the trees, not wanting to overtake them during the night, or lose their trail.

They saddled up and pulled out twenty minutes later, fording the swift-moving stream, climbing up on the far bank and riding as quickly as the terrain allowed. Halfway through the morning, with the heat head lifting to almost intolerable heights, they came down from the tall ridge, out into a wide, shallow basin that stretched for the best part of two miles ahead of them before the further rim lifted thirty or forty feet into the air. The floor of the basin was sandy and dry, the trail scarcely seen as they picked their way across it. Here and there, it was dotted with tall boulders which they skirted carefully, keeping a sharp eye open for any razor-edged gulches which could snap a horse's leg and throw a man hard enough to break his neck.

Kearney sat stiffly in the saddle, easing one leg at a time. He had slept badly through the night, not sure, in spite of his outward confidence that Denver was not closing in on them more quickly than they figured. Twisting and turning, he had rolled in his blankets from side to side on the rough, stony ground so that now he was stiff and sorer in his limbs than he had been the previous day. He wiped the sweat from his brow, pulled the canteen from where it hung at the saddlehorn, uncorked it, and swallowed greedily. Woodrow rode a little distance ahead of him, silent and trail-grimed like himself. For a while, Kearney studied the other's back, tried to figure out what they would do if they ever managed to get as far as the California border. But curiously, his mind refused to project itself as far ahead as that; as though it recognised the inescapable fact that there lay no hope in that direction. He knew a little too much about Jeff Denver really to believe that the other would ever give up trailing them. The anger and the need for revenge that was riding Denver was too much for him ever to think of turning back. He would follow them across an entire continent to finish his chore.

For a moment, he wondered briefly if it would be possible to make a deal with Denver should he catch up with them. Maybe offer to go back east and testify to the truth of what had actually happened. True there was no longer any Confederate Army to whom such a confession could be made, but it might be enough to satisfy Denver if they were able to arrange the records. But almost as soon as he had thought of that, he rejected the idea. Denver would want not only revenge for what had happened to him, but also for those men who had been killed in the trap that had been laid for him.

He wondered if Woodrow had ever considered this, opened his mouth to ask, then tightened his grip convulsively on the reins as his horse shied, then reared up into the air with a frightened squeal. Surprised, he stared down at the trail, trying to make out what had scared the animal so much. Then he saw the cause of the trouble. The rattler lay in a small hollow where they had undoubtedly disturbed it. It was coiled, head reared back, poised to strike. Savagely, he jerked the Colt from its holster, aimed a snap shot at the snake. The bullet struck the sand within an inch of its body, but instead of frightening the reptile off, it merely served to enrage it even more. The horse lashed out with its feet, then leapt four-footed into the air, unseating Kearney. He hit the ground hard, rolled over swiftly, cursing, fear coursing through him. His gun was out, swinging desperately as he strove to bring it to bear on the rattler. Woodrow had heard the commotion, had stopped and was turning his mount. He took in the situation in a single glance, levelled his own gun and fired.

On the ground, Kearney tried to heave himself to his feet but the snake, slithering forward in a blur of colour, sank its fangs into his leg, just above the ankle. Again it struck, teeth sinking harmlessly into Kearney's boot. Before it could jerk back its head to strike again, Woodrow's gun thundered once more and the slug cut the reptile in half.

Sliding from the saddle, Woodrow came forward, holstered his gun, then went down on one knee. 'Did it hit you?' he asked tightly.

Wincing, Kearney nodded, teeth gritted as the full enormity of the situation penetrated his dulled mind. He could feel the numbness in his leg, knew that unless something was done quickly the poison would spread through his veins and he would be dead within an hour or so.

'Hold still,' muttered the other rapidly. He drew his knife from his belt, slit Kearney's pants at the bottom of the leg, revealing the twin punctures which were already flaring an angry red.

'This won't be nice,' he gritted harshly.

'Go ahead,' muttered the other. 'I know what you've got to do.'

Swiftly, Woodrow made a deep cut across the two punctures, letting the blood flow freely. Then, bending, he commenced to suck the blood and spit it out on to the sand until he felt certain that most of the poison had been removed. There was nothing more he could do but make a tourniquet of his bandana and tighten it around Kearney's leg just above the knee. Whether this fragile job of surgery had been effective was something neither of them knew.

'How does it feel now?'

Kearney sucked in a sharp gust of air. 'Numb,' he said thinly. He stared out across the sandy floor of the basin, squinting as the shimmering waves of heat and light made his head ache. The throbbing pain of his own blood as it pounded at the back of his eyes brought a wave of sickness through him. 'It'll be all right once I get back into the saddle. Reckon you can help me up?'

Woodrow nodded, took the other's weight against his shoulder and helped him over to the horse. It took him several moments to get the other into the saddle and even then it was painfully obvious that he would not be able to hold on for long.

Conquering the increasing sensation of sickness that threatened to overwhelm him, Kearney struggled to remain in the saddle. It would be all right if only the heat wasn't so bad and everything stopped spinning around in front of his stultified vision. The swaying motion of the horse through this loose, drifting sand was hell though. Why the devil couldn't it walk properly? He forced himself to screw up his eyes against the terrible glare. In front of him, holding the reins in one hand, Woodrow was a dimly blurred figure, just seen through waves of sickness. A few moments later, he was surprised to find himself lying on his side in the hot sand, his horse standing patiently a few feet sway. Woodrow was bending over him, holding the neck of his canteen to his lips, letting the water trickle slowly down his throat.

There were waves of agony lancing along his leg now and it felt as though it was swollen to twice its normal size. Desperately he tried to move it, felt the cold wash of fear in his mind as he realised that it was impossible for him to do so.

'What in hell's name happened?' he asked weakly.

'You fell out of the saddle,' muttered Woodrow. He corked the canteen, then laid it carefully in the sand near Kearney's left hand. Getting to his feet he stood looking down at the other and there was no expression on his face.

'What's the matter?' Kearney stared up at the other, blinking his eyes against the glare of the sun. 'Why are you lookin' at me like that?'

Woodrow said nothing, but let the silence build up, then turned and moved away in the direction of his horse. Looking back, he said harshly, speaking through tightly-clenched teeth, 'You could never make it, Reno. Don't you realise that? Denver could be here soon and I don't mean to let him catch me just because you can't—'

'You're not leavin' me here, dammit!'

Woodrow said flatly: 'This is the partin' of the ways for us, Reno. You've got to face up to the facts of life. Denver is on our trail and you ain't in no fit condition to keep up with me. Reckon you'd better even the score with him when he comes this way. By the time he gets past you, I figure I should be well clear of the State and on my way into California.' He swung up into the saddle, jerked hard on the reins and set his mount at a swift canter across the basin floor. For several minutes Reno struggled to get to his feet, watching the other head off into the sun-hazed distance. Anger was the first emotion that took hold of his mind and in spite of the pain in his body and the weakness he struggled to his feet and stood swaying for a moment, aware of the shock waves of pain that seared through his leg and up into his body. Woodrow was far off in the distance now, too far away to hear him if he shouted and he knew he would have to conserve all of his strength if he was to remain conscious. There was a tumbled heap of boulders in the middle of the smooth, sandy floor and he dragged his way over to it, sank down in the meagre shadow of one of them, drew his Colt from its holster and checked that all of the chambers were full before lying down on his stomach, peering into the distance, in the direction from which he expected Denver to come.

The sun lifted higher into the cloudless, brassy heavens. The shadows shortened until there were none at all and the entire floor of the basin drowned in the blistering heat of high noon. At times, he lapsed into unconsciousness, his head falling forward on to his arms and he knew nothing until the pain forced him back to reality once more and he cursed himself, and then cursed Woodrow for leaving him like this. Through red-rimmed eyes, he peered into the heat haze, scanning the far rim of the basin, trying to make out any indication of a dust cloud which would pick out for him the position of a rider approaching along the trail, but the minutes ticked by, lengthening into a heat-filled eternity, when he floated on a hazy sea of numbing pain, and still there was no sign of Denver. He forced himself to accept the fact that the other might not arrive here for days, all depending on when he discovered that they had left Marsden's place and he knew, with a deepening sense of dread, that he would be dead long before then, if not from the snake venom, then from hunger and thirst.

CHAPTER 8

GUNSMOKE RETRIBUTION

Jeff came upon the basin during the early afternoon. The blistering heat was fierce now, the sun blazing down from a cloudless sky and in the depression ahead of him there was no breeze. The air stood still and hot, as if it had been pulled over some vast furnace and then left there. He reined up among the narrow fringe of trees that skirted the natural basin. Far up in the brassy heavens, he noticed the flock of zopilote buzzards, wheeling slowly and with an eerie singleness of purpose that told its own story.

Narrowing down his lids, he stared across the depression, seeking the reason for the buzzards' presence there. Had Kearney and Woodrow met up with some unfortunate rider here, killed him for his money? It was a possible reason, one he could not dismiss from his calculations. On the other hand, he could see nothing out there which gave him cause for apprehension. Then he caught the sudden movement far off on the other side of the basin. It was a horse, moving slowly but apparently unharmed, riderless.

Puzzled, he tried to figure out what could have

happened. Few men ever used this trail. There was a perfectly good stage route further to the north which skirted around this bad country and was used almost exclusively. Only those on the run ever came here. Had the two men quarrelled? That was a definite possibility. Both had quick tempers and it was likely that these would be frayed by the knowledge that he might be close behind them, closing in on them.

He debated for a few more minutes and then put his horse to the downgrade and rode into the sandy basin. Boring steadily forward, he kept his eyes and ears open, watchful and alert, his right hand never straying very far from the gun at this hip.

He was almost halfway across the basin when the single gunshot rang out with a sudden crash of sound. Instinctively, Jeff dropped from the saddle, hit the ground and rolled over, lying quite still. The bullet had missed him by less than a foot and he cast about him for the tell-tale puff of smoke, hanging in the still air, that would give away the position of the dry-gulcher. He spotted it a moment later, hanging over the clump of rocks in the middle of the basin floor. Tightening his lips, he waited.

He studied the terrain thoughtfully, lips pursed. He was slightly higher than the other's position because of the lie of the ground in the centre of the depression. Beyond the rocks there was more open ground and he reckoned that the other would not try to make it over that ground and to his mount. Probably he's been hurt in some way and he knows he'll never make it, Jeff thought inwardly. He could have been thrown by his horse and hurt and once the horse had bolted there would have been no chance for him to catch it again; but if that was the case, then where was the other member of the duo? Surely he hadn't just ridden off and left his companion to fight it out alone – yet it certainly seemed like it. Unless it was a trap, to draw his attention while the other sneaked up on him from behind. He gave an uneasy look over his shoulder, keeping his head well down, but there seemed to be no possible way by which anyone could come up on him from that direction without being seen a half mile away.

He aimed quickly at the spot where he had seen the gunsmoke, fired two shots, one on either side of the place, heard the slugs whine off the solid rock into the distance with the high-pitched shriek of tortured metal.

There was no reply from the other. Evidently, he was not going to waste any lead on shooting at a target he could not see properly. He would wait until Jeff was forced to show himself.

Keeping his body pressed tightly against the sun-baked sand, he wriggled along to his right, circling around the other. There was a small clump of rocks a short distance away, but when he reached them he could still make out no sign of the gunman. Better try to move a little more around, he reflected and if possible, a little closer. Getting his legs under him, he thrust off, running a short distance and then dropping flat in a shallow depression in the sand. The Colt opened up once more, the bullets slapping into the dirt at his heels and he hurled himself horizontally the last couple of yards. He hit the dirt hard, lay gasping for a moment with all of the wind knocked out of his lungs. The Colt came up with his head as he covered the rocks now less than thirty yards away.

Reno! He caught a brief glimpse of the other's face, ducking down among the rocks. So that was who the dry-gulcher had been. He might have guessed. This was Reno's speciality. Shooting a man down from cover without giving him an even break. He grinned viciously as the realisation came to him. But where was Woodrow?

Quickly, he called: 'You don't have a chance, Reno. Better come on out. If you don't, I'll come in after you.'

'You'll kill me anyway, Denver,' yelled the other. 'So you're goin' to have to do it the hard way. I ain't budgin' from here, no matter what you say.'

'What happened to Woodrow? He ride off and leave you here?'

'I don't need that yeller-bellied coward to help me, Denver; and you know it.'

Jeff leaned over on to his side, thumbed fresh shells into the empty chambers and nodded slowly to himself. The other's remark told him all he needed to know. For some reason, Woodrow had run out on Reno, had left him in the lurch. He could imagine the other feeling bitter about it, was vaguely surprised that Reno had not taken him up on his offer to step out with his hands lifted.

Behind the rocks, Jeff settled down to wait. He had the feeling that time was on his side as far as Reno Kearney was concerned. The other was hurt – how badly he did not know, but long before the sun went down, Kearney was going to make a move and when he did, Jeff intended to be ready for him. He settled his back and shoulders against the hot rock, made himself a smoke. Lighting it, he drew the tobacco smoke deeply into his lungs.

'You still there, Denver? Skulking behind those rocks?'

Jeff grinned to himself in the harsh sunlight. The other was beginning to feel the strain. His voice had been slurred and the syllables were all run together. He said nothing, content to wait it out.

'I said are you still there?' The other was working himself up into something approaching a frenzy. 'You're as big a coward as Woodrow.'

Now the strain was really beginning to tell on the other. Squinting up at the glaring disc of the sun, he decided that it was now time for him to make a move. He pressed himself flat to the ground, holding the Colt straight out in front of him at arm's length, moving forward with heaving motions of his legs. He could hear the other muttering something to himself under his breath but it was not possible to make out the words. He seemed to be speaking in a delirium and it came to Jeff that perhaps he had been badly hurt and the heat and sickening glare had already taken its inevitable toll of him.

He reached a spot almost level with the rocks behind which the other lay hidden. Screwing up his eyes as the sunlight threatened to blind him, he caught a glimpse of Reno's legs thrust out on the sandy earth. He could not make out the rest of the other's body, but this was enough for him.

Carefully, he sighted his gun on the ground just behind Reno. If possible he wanted to take the other alive. There were some questions he wanted to ask and only Reno could give him the answers.

He squeezed off the single shot, the wheeling buzzards flapping their wings at the bucketing echoes that chased themselves over the flat floor of the basin. He saw the bullet strike the earth where he had intended, saw Reno's body jerk and twitch, saw his head come up in sudden surprise.

'Just hold it right there, Reno,' he called loudly 'and toss out your gun or the next slug gets you in the back. I'll give you five seconds to make up your mind.'

'Damn your hide, Denver,' snarled the other. He twisted over on to his side. Jeff caught the flash of sunlight on the blued barrel of the other's gun, fired without hesitation and saw Reno fall back as the slug hit him in the side.

The gun in the other's hand tilted, a single shot was squeezed off, ploughing into the earth a couple of feet in front of the outlaw. Then the gun fell from his fingers. Getting cautiously to his feet, Jeff went forward. A moment later, he stood over the dying man, staring down at him with a faint sense of surprise. One look at the other's stiff leg told him all he needed to know of what had happened.

'What was it – a rattlesnake?' he asked.

The other stared up at him through pain-filled eyes, eyes that were dulling already. He nodded, the muscles of his throat constricting.

'And Woodrow decided to leave you here to get what was comin' to you. Not the sort of companion I'd trust.'

Through thinned lips, Reno said: 'He rode out on me when he saw I'd be a hindrance to him. Guess he was scared you'd catch up with us and we wouldn't have a chance so he decided to save his own skin.'

'Where is he now?' Jeff bent beside the other. He noticed the look of pain slowly slip away from the man's face, saw the dark shadows deepen under the sunken eyes and knew that the end was very near. He saw the stain of blood on his side, but he knew that it was not his bullet that had killed the other. The snake poison was still inside his body in spite of the attempt that had been made to suck it out of the wound. It was this, more than anything else, which was killing him.

'He's headed out for California. Maybe he figured you wouldn't be along for some days and I'd die of thirst.'

'How much start has he got?'

'Not much. Three hours or so. Can't be much more.' The other's voice faltered and the greyness came to his face, the flesh sinking down on to the bone structure. His head fell back as he tried to lift it. Reaching out for the other's canteen, he shook it, heard the water splash inside it and uncorked it, placing it to the other's lips. The water trickled down the other's throat and then he lay back, a long sigh escaping from him.

His eyes, which had been closed, flickered suddenly open and Jeff saw to his surprise that all of the pain and dullness had been miraculously washed away. 'Reckon you've got plenty of reason for wantin' me dead, Denver. Can't say I blame you after what happened. Always knew you'd catch up with us someday no matter how far we tried to run.'

'Wasn't me who finished you, Reno. Reckon you know that.'

145

'I know. That goddamned snake. If it hadn't been for that rattler we'd have been miles away from here by now and you might never have caught us.' The other's voice faded so that Jeff had to strain to catch the last words. Then Reno swallowed thickly, waited for a moment, then went on: 'Those buzzards up there, Denver. Guess you know what they're waitin' for. Want you to do me one last favour. Know I ain't got the right to ask it, but put some stones on top of me, just to keep them and the coyotes away. I—' He gave a sudden gasp, his body jerked in some kind of spasm, his back arching. Then he sank down again, lay still, his last breath gone from his body.

Jeff got slowly to his feet. He no longer felt any hate for the dead man. All of that was wiped away now. The slate was clean as far as Reno Kearney was concerned.

He spent almost an hour digging a hole in the hard earth, then piling some of the larger rocks on top of the shallow grave. When he had finished, the sun was lowering westward. Wiping the sweat from his face, he walked back to his horse. Turning his face towards the reddening sun, he rode slowly towards the misty horizon, riding loosely and with little spirit. He had figured that with Reno's death, there would be a feeling of elation in avenging those men who had died because of the other's treachery and actions; but there was nothing like that, only a curious emptiness which he had not experienced since that terrible morning when all of those men had died in the withering fire from the Yankee ambush.

He rode slowly, strangely conscious that he would, sooner or later, meet up with Matt Woodrow. How he was so certain of this, he did not know. But every man had the feeling at some time in his life that a certain course of events was going to take place and that nothing he could do would prevent it, or change it in the slightest degree. That was how Jeff Denver felt as he swayed with his mount in the cooling breeze of the dying day.

*

For the first time in his life, Matt Woodrow was really afraid. From the moment he had ridden out of that basin, knowing that he was leaving Reno to his death, he had not felt right. It was not a remorse of conscience, rather a chill sense of premonition, a warning that Reno's fate would soon be his own and there was little he could do about it. The knowledge came to him when he paused two mornings later on a high rise of ground and turned to look back along the trail. The cloud of dust near the horizon where the trail wound out of thick timber was no bigger than a man's hand, but it told him all that he had feared.

He did not need to think to know that it was Denver riding on his trail, coming closer all the time, edging up on him. Inwardly, he knew it would not be possible for him to reach the comparative sanctuary of the border. He would have to make his stand somewhere along the trail and his own life was going to depend on making the right decision, because with a man like Denver, he would never get a second chance.

There was a faint, but persistent pale greyness off to the east and he turned his back on it and kicked savagely at his mount's flanks, urging it along the trail. It was tired, wanted to have its own head, protested when he refused to allow it, but he raked spurs cruelly along its sides. The morning slowly brightened. The light to the east passed through an entire spectrum of colours and then the sun came up, bringing with it the beginning of the warmth. He felt it on his back and shoulders and in spite of it, a shiver went through him. Goddamn that Reno, he thought angrily. He had been able to set up an ambush for Denver and yet he had somehow made a mess of that. Maybe though Reno had been dead when Denver had reached the basin.

With an effort, he shrugged the idea from his mind,

concentrated on methods of saving his own life. That was the most important thing now. He cast his gaze ahead of him, searching the terrain for a suitable spot where he might rein up and wait for Denver to come. Gritting his teeth, he thought: 'This time there won't be any mistake. This time, it'll be Denver who dies.'

The thought stayed with him as he rode quickly, through stretches of pine and over rocky gulches. Here, the country was all broken up into ledges and ridges, bubbling creeks that raced across the trail, water splashing against his horse's chest as he put it across the surging current.

He moved up out of the canyons and arroyos. Here there was more open country lying ahead of him and the knowledge gave him pause. Once he was out there in the desert, he stood very little chance of laying up a trap for Denver. It would have to be here, where there was plenty of cover for him.

Moving off the trail he entered the trees, found a grassy clearing on the edge of the track and dismounted. He reckoned that Denver was an hour or so behind him. That gave him little time to set up something, but the knowledge that he was as good as dead if he didn't, spurred him on.

From the deep and endless quiet of the forest all about him, he traced the faint sound of the approaching rider, listening to his cautious, onward progress. From his vantage point, he was able to look down through the lower branches of the trees below him and see the trail at intermittent points. He took the Winchester from its scabbard, then settled himself down behind a deadfall to wait, the rifle propped in front of him. Slowly, forcing casualness into his every action, he took out his tobacco pouch and made himself a cigarette. A little nerve began to twitch in his chest in spite of the tight control he forced on himself.

For a second, far off beyond one of the ridges, he

caught sight of horse and rider moving along the trail. Denver was advancing slowly, taking no chances. Woodrow felt certain that as soon as the other became aware of the changing terrain in front of him, he would know instantly that he was lying in wait for him here, that he would not have attempted to move out over the desert.

He grinned viciously in the pale green gloom. He would need only one shot at Denver, just the one, and it would be all over. He would continue his journey to California and there would be nothing else for him to fear. For too long, Denver had been on his trail. It had been utterly impossible to forget him altogether.

He was surprised at the slowness with which Denver came on but comforted himself with the knowledge that he held the advantage. The other, if he stuck to the trail, would present an excellent target when he was still some distance away and the Winchester was a very accurate weapon. Gradually, he began to feel a little easier in his mind, more confident of the outcome of the impending encounter.

He shifted himself into a more comfortable position, squinted along the sights of the rifle, staring along the V until it was lined up on the furthest position he could see along the trail. The minutes passed, dragging themselves into the deep stillness. He could still make out the sound of the other's horse, pacing its steady way along the trail. At least, the other had not moved away from the trail as he had half expected. Had Denver done that, he would have been faced with the dilemma of trying to spot him again in the brush.

Very quietly, carbine steady in both hands, his finger on the trigger, he waited. The other was quite close now. He could pick out the measured echoes of the horse's hoofs on the rocky trail. A moment later, it came out into an open stretch of ground where he could just make it out through the swaying branches of the trees.

The horse was riderless. Even as the realisation penetrated Woodrow's mind, his awareness of the danger of his position came to him in a rush of cold fear. In hell's name why hadn't he considered this possibility earlier? He cursed harshly under his breath, switching his glance from the trail to the sea of greenness about him.

Denver had been too clever for him. The other must have realised that he would stop and fight here and he had slipped from the saddle while he was still out of sight and he had allowed his horse to move slowly along the trail, while he had moved off into the undergrowth and was, at that very moment, probably closing in on him.

Desperately, he searched about him with eyes and ears, knowing that he had no chance at all of beating Denver to the draw in an even fight, that his only hope lay in taking the other by surprise. Now, it seemed, all of his carefully laid plans had gone wrong.

Jeff Denver moved down the slope slowly, making no sound in the thick, spongy earth beneath the trees. Woodrow was running scared and he had known, the instant he had seen the flat desert stretching away to the distant horizon, that the other would never risk crossing it. Not with him so close behind him. If he'd thought he had a good start, he might have chanced it. Now, he was lying in wait somewhere among the trees, probably with a Winchester lined up on the trail, his finger itching to put a bullet into him the instant he showed himself within killing range of the weapon.

The move of slipping from the saddle without the horse breaking its stride and sending it on along the trail, was one he had learned during the war, but evidently it had worked this time. He wondered what thoughts must have crossed Woodrow's mind the moment he saw the horse come into view with nobody in the saddle.

Parting the bushes in front of him, ignoring the

sharply-pointed thorns that raked across the backs of his hands, drawing blood, he found himself staring at Woodrow's back, less than fifty yards away, crouching down behind a fallen tree, his rifle resting on the trunk in front of him. Judging from the other's uneasy movements, he had guessed what had happened and he was now more afraid than ever. Jeff crouched, rock still, for several moments, keeping his eye on the other.

A frightened man had sharp ears. All of his senses were stretched to the limit. He knew better than to move out and take Woodrow from behind. Let him stew for a while, he figured. Pretty soon if he didn't make a move, the strain was going to get the better of him.

Jeff remained where he was for a long time, watching the other, his eyes taking in every little movement. It was clear that Woodrow was apprehensively shaken. Inwardly, Jeff felt a faint flush of triumph. This was what he had been waiting for, for so long that it had seemed a part of him, something which had always been there. But it was not in him to shoot the other in the back without a chance to defend himself, although it was no more than the other deserved. It was a better chance than he had given any of those men who had been cut down by that withering hail of fire from well-prepared positions.

The thinking along these lines brought a hint of cruelty to his face, a tight set to his jaw line. Woodrow was more nervous now. He began to edge along the deadfall, bobbing his head up and down as he squinted along the trail. The silence too was beginning to eat at his nerves like acid.

While the other's back was turned towards him, Jeff straightened, stepped out of the bushes and moved swiftly over the open ground. He stopped when he was twenty feet from the other, said in a harsh, thin voice: 'Woodrow. If you value your life, hold it right there and don't try to use that rifle!'

Woodrow's shoulder blades twitched, but he did not turn and he did not remove his hand from the butt of the rifle which lay in front of him.

'That you, Denver?' he asked in a thin tone, the words edged with strain.

'You're darned right it is. Now are you goin' to let go that rifle, toss down your handgun and lift your hands or not?'

'And if I do?'

'Then I'm takin' you back into Culver Creek to stand trial for murder.'

Woodrow uttered a harsh, barking laugh. 'That's a good one, Denver. You reckon you can take me in with that story. You'd shoot me in the back long before we got anywhere in sight of the town. It would be easy for you, wouldn't it. Say that I was shot tryin' to escape.'

'If I wanted to shoot you in the back, I'd have done it from back there,' Denver said pointedly.

'Maybe.' The other shifted his legs. 'Or maybe it's some trick. You want it to look like I was tryin' somethin' when I got shot. That way you could salve your own conscience. It won't allow you to shoot me down in cold blood, but given a tiny excuse like that, is enough for you.'

'You're forgettin' that I saw you watchin' that trail with that rifle. You'd have shot me down without warnin' like the yellow snake you are.'

Jeff gave a mirthless grin. He said shortly, 'Then if that's the way you feel about this, use that rifle. Either do that, or drop it. I'll give you ten seconds.'

'What happened to Reno? Did you give him the same kind of chance?'

'The snake bite killed him, not me.'

'I don't believe you.' Woodrow eased himself a little off the ground. 'Still if you give me your word that you won't kill me in cold blood, I'll—'

Woodrow had been banking on his words lulling Jeff

into a state of false security. He swung swiftly, sharply, bringing up the barrel of the rifle as he did so. He made no attempt to go for the Colt in its holster. Instead, he banked every thing on shooting Jeff down before the other could reach his gun. How he had guessed that it was in the holster, Jeff did not know. But with the sudden warning flash inside his head, his right hand moved in a blur of speed, striking downward for his gun.

The twin muzzle blasts sounded loudly and almost together, blending in a roll of sound. Jeff felt the slug burn its way along his arm, tearing into the flesh. The gun dropped from fingers which could no longer hold it.

In front of him, Woodrow lay with his back against the deadfall. There was a thin, tight-lipped grin on his face as he stared up at Jeff. He opened his mouth to speak, but a bubbling gush of red came out and his fingers moved up instinctively, touching the red stain on the front of his shirt, covering the ugly hole.

Bending, Jeff touched him on the shoulder, but the other fell away from him, toppling over on to his side. He straightened up, glanced down at the wound in his arm. The slug had ploughed through the flesh but did not seem to have touched the bone. He was going to have a stiff and painful arm for a while.

Moving down through the trees, he reached the trail and whistled up his mount. There was nothing left for him to do here and he headed east back into the rocks.

Three days later, he rode down from the low hills. Ahead of him lay Culver Creek, a faint blotch of shadow in the distance. He flexed his stiff arm, loosened the strip of cloth which he had wound about it, moved his fingers experimentally. It still pained him a little but most of the feeling had come back into his hand and arm.

He felt dehydrated and tired as he rode through the low rocks. Beyond that was another feeling, curiously apprehensive and more unpleasant. He had been away from here for almost a week now, riding that vengeance trail and for all he knew, Marsden could have carried out his threat and brought in more of the desert crew to build up his force and impose his own kind of law on the territory.

The moon lifted as he rode into the wide street, flooding everything in a cold, white radiance. The bitter smell of dust hung heavy in the air and as he rode, he tried to gauge the feel of the town. Very often a man could guess at what had happened in his absence by the atmosphere in town. Now he sensed something a little different. There no longer seemed to be that apprehension hanging over everything.

There was a yellow light showing in the sheriff's office and he reined up outside, then went in, closing the door behind him. Sheriff Block Parker was seated in the chair at the desk, his feet up, his hat drawn down over his face. He was snoring so loudly that he did not hear the other come in, grunted harshly as Jeff jerked him by the shoulder. Bending, Jeff pushed back the other's hat and Parker opened his eyes, blinking them in the yellow lamplight. He licked his lips, squinted up at Jeff, then swung his feet sharply off the desk.

'When in tarnation did you get back into town, Denver?' he asked. 'Last I heard you'd ridden out to Marsden's place and then headed west after two of his boys.'

'Those were the two men I'd been trailin',' Jeff told him. He noticed the can of coffee on the stove in the corner of the room, went over and poured himself a mug full. He sipped it slowly, letting some of the warmth come back into his body.

'You get 'em?' Parker inquired, eyeing him with a bright-sharp stare.

'I got them. Both of the critters,' Jeff nodded. He

154

finished the coffee in deep, noisy gulps.

'You look as if you've been hit yourself,' observed the other, nodding towards Jeff's arm.

'That's nothin' but a flesh wound. It'll heal up in a day or two. But what's been happenin' around here since I've been away? Marsden was swearin' he'd bring in more of the desert crew and smash the nesters once and for all.'

Parker sat back in his chair, pushed his hat further back on his head. He grinned broadly. 'That was his intention. You really busted up his crew that night you trapped most of 'em in the valley. He rode into town the very next mornin', ordered me to get a posse together, ride out and arrest Fenner and the Sheddens.'

''So that was where he was headed in such an all-fired hurry.'

Parker nodded. 'I told him that I'd have to wire through to Dallas and get word from the Governor, since the nesters had apparently got themselves a lawyer to petition him on their behalf. I reckon that must've shaken him up real bad. Guess it must have made him realise that he didn't have a chance with the Governor gettin' to hear about this little matter. Strengthened my hand anyway.'

'So what did he do then?'

Parker shrugged. 'Last I heard, he was back at the ranch, but most of the rest of his boys have ridden out. Word got around that the State Governor was takin' an interest in Marsden's activities hereabouts and since most of them were wanted by the law in some State or other, they figured they would no longer get the protection he'd promised them in the beginning.' Parker leaned forward, resting his weight on his elbows. 'You know, I figure this could be the beginnin' of somethin' a heap better for Culver Creek and the surroundin' territory.'

'I hope you're right. It has to come someday, but whether it'll be now or later is goin' to depend a lot on the ordinary folk around these parts. In particular, on how they react to the homesteaders. These folk are goin' to move in soon in ever-increasin' numbers. They'll really make this State. But we've all got to learn to live with 'em. The longer we try to fight 'em as Marsden and the others did, then the longer it's goin' to be before this place grows up and takes its rightful place in the territory.'

Parker gave a quick nod. He eyed Jeff closely. 'And what about you, Denver? What do you figure on doin' now that your chore is finished? Ride on out, or stay here and maybe put down roots in this town?'

'You won't want a man who's been court-martialled from the Army with dishonour,' Jeff said quietly.

Parker shrugged again. 'Could be that there's somebody who might make you change your mind on that point. I was talkin' to Susan Fenner yesterday when she rode into town for supplies.' He sighed melodramatically. 'Only wish that I was a dozen years younger myself.' He looked wistfully in front of him as Jeff got to his feet.

'What was she sayin'?' Jeff asked a few moments later.

'Oh, nothin' in particular. just that she reckoned you might be able to stop runnin' if you finished your chore with these *hombres*. She seems to think a lot of you, Denver. If I was you, I'd have a wash and a bath, and then ride out to the Fenner place. Unless you'd prefer to ride on west, of course.'

He sank back into his chair as he realised that he was now talking to the empty air. The street door swung shut a moment later.

An hour later, Jeff rode east down the star-strewn night, with the round face of the moon climbing slowly in the south-east. It glowed a soft silver in the night, lighting the trail that led him over the valley and then through the rolling flatness of the desert.

When he rode through the narrow pass into the valley that lay beyond, past the scene of so much violence a week or so before, the moon threw long shadows over the rocks so that they stood out starkly in black and white. He rode past the Sheddens' place, saw far off the homestead that was being built by the family which had just arrived. Yes, he thought to himself as he felt the cool night air on his face, it was going to be some country this once they got their backs into it.

Ahead of him, the Fenner place glowed with pale light in its windows. He rode past the neat squares of cultivated ground, past the patch of alfalfa which he had noticed on that day when he had first come here. All that seemed a long age ago, almost as if it had happened in another world. For a moment as he reined up in the small courtyard, he felt more at a loss than at any other time in his life. He wondered if he was doing right coming here like this, wondered if—

The door opened and he saw a slender figure outlined against the lamp glow, the yellow light softening the contours of her body.

'I heard your horse off in the distance,' said Susan, stepping towards him down the steps. 'I guessed it might be you – I mean I hoped that it would be.' She came to a gradual halt a few paces from him as he dropped from the saddle, her face a pale blur in the moonlight. Then he stepped forward, touched her, felt the warmth of her under his fingers, drew her towards him. The pressure of her hands, drawing his head down told him everything he needed to know.